TWO
PEAS
Jamal Brown

"Two Peas"
The Assignment: Pass or Fail

Written By
Jamal Brown

"TWO PEAS"
THE ASSIGNMENT: PASS OR FAIL

Published by Jamal Brown
dba BrotherBrown Publishing

Pre-Press Book Preparation by Proven Publishing
www.provenpublishing.com

Cover Design by Jess Paul Art (jesspaulart.com)
Layout by Proven Publishing (provenpublishing.com)

First Printing 2020

LCCN: 2020900558   ISBN 13: **978-8-9928804-0-3**

3

This book is dedicated to the underdog. I know you have big dreams that scare you out of even attempting to manifest them sometimes. I have swum in those emotions before. I pray you escape your stress pool and find a towel and dry off. I know it's hard to get support from the people you love the most. Believe me, I know. Please don't stop pursuing whatever you are trying to create. The world needs it. Matter of fact, I need it. The world is always late to catch on to great things. Put the work in and I will meet you at the top. Life is a marathon. Still We Run.

-Brother Brown

DEDICATION

To **Walter Brown III**, you were my biggest critic when it came to writing books. I made it my life's task to prove to you that I can write and be successful at it. May you continue to Rest in Peace. I love you and miss you dearly.

To my **Grandmother**, who loves me unconditionally no matter what! Your love and prayers have kept me alive and sane through all my hard times. Love you forever.

To **Melissa**, I hope this book bridges the gap of understanding between the two worlds we were raised in.

To my **Mother**: Thanks for all the unconditional love. I know you want me to win and make you proud. Let me show you on my own terms. I promise I won't let you down.

To the **Huntsmen**: Thanks for the health and wellness checks throughout the creation of this book. I still owe you both that vacation. Hold me to it.

To **Brother Sunflower and Slick Rick**: Forever my dogs, you two will always remain in my left tit.

To my two brothers **Jamil** and **Tre**: My brothers for life. When life was rough, and the world had its foot on my neck, thanks for the talks. You two helped me in ways I can't explain.

To **Yesenia**: May my perseverance through life be a guide to help you heal as you run your marathon. Keep running.

To **Supreme Understanding**: thanks for all the information you shared with me. I will analyze it and create something great! Never stop teaching. The world needs you! Peace.

To **Javon:** For the support during a pivotal transition in my life. Thank you.

To **Curtis**: for keeping me updated on the game and all that comes with it. I live through you. Never stop living, kid. You are #BrotherBrown approved!

To **Mama Maynard**: Thanks for the unconditional love and support in all my endeavors.

To my **Trauma**: The experiences we have shared throughout my life have formed a short novel. I am thankful for the lessons.

To the **Reader**: Thank you for your purchase. I hope you enjoy this work of art and learn something.

"For anything illegal, there is a legal side to it
Get in and get out
Kings don't live long where we're from
Check the scoreboard"

-Brother Brown

Table of Contents

INTRODUCTION
(THE ASSIGNMENT)

Dozing in and out of consciousness, I struggle to stay awake in my psychology class. I hate this class with a passion. I am tired of listening to the voice of my teacher. I rarely come to this class, to begin with, that's why I have an F now. I heard we have a test today. That is the only reason for my presence.

Dr. Banks is a boring lecturer. He sees my head nod back and forth and wakes me up. He instructs me to see him after class. My classmates laugh and throw paper at me.

Ten minutes later. The bell rings.

I stroll up to Dr. Banks' desk. My stomach is in knots as I approach his desk. I don't know what to expect. He pulls out a sheet of paper.

"I'm sorry for sleeping in class sir, I have a lot going on at the moment in my personal life."

"Son, you have barely come to class this marking period. You are at risk of flunking. The only way you can pass this class is if you complete a special assignment I have created."

He hands me the assignment.

It read:

"Death is the price we pay for living. When humans die they usually give birth to their legacies. When you pass on, what will be your story? How will you be remembered? There is a war going on inside each and every one of us. Two people reside in you. The true you and the person you reveal to the world. They constantly clash as they both battle to rule your perception. This battle has been going on since the beginning of time."

Assignment: Write a story portraying the clash within you. You say you have a lot going on in your personal life. You say you are also misunderstood in all aspects as well. Help me understand to the best of your ability. Use your imagination. I am a tough critic, so you better wow me son. Help me understand the thoughts that young men deal with on a daily basis in this day and age. Bridge the gap of communication between our two generations.

Be descriptive. This is a PASS or FAIL assignment. This will be due next week. Good luck.

"Everything we hear is an opinion, not a fact. Everything we see is a perspective, not the truth.
                    -Marcus Aurelius

Damn. Now I have to type this stupid paper because I was absent one too many times. Whelp here goes nothing. I hope I pass. I hope he understands.

Chapter 1:
THE HILL

I can't help where I come from, but while I am here I will make the best of it until I get to where I am going. Adversity builds character and I can use that as a shield to stay away from trouble.

-Brother Brown

Loud music plays from a big speaker. "Can I Live" by Jay Z is the current tune. Illegal transactions are being conducted as cars pull up and drive off quickly. The wind is cutting through all layers of clothing. Candy wrappers, empty potato chip bags, and beer bottles cover the grass patches in front of the project buildings. Small kids play catch with a football on the sidewalk. The sounds of police sirens are heard in the distance. The patrons of this community wear masks of despair. The world has gotten the best of them. Where am I? I am in Bridgeton, New Jersey. In the midst of this poverty-stricken area, resides a righteous young king who is slowly rising through the ranks.

Peace. Welcome to my world. My name is Dre Peters, but everyone calls me "Knowledge". I live in Bridgeton, NJ. We call it "Money Bridge" due to the town being home to some of the best hustlers. I'm the neighborhood basketball star and I have the grades to back it up. At sixteen, I am the total package. I am an avid reader being raised by both parents who have heavy ties to The Black Panther Party. I guess you can say I am disciplined. We live in a rough part of town called "The Hill". I am an only child.

My best friend is Pain. He lives next door to me. He is the neighborhood drug dealer, always fly and flashy. He runs the Cobras, a ruthless gang in the town. Pain is always focused on his money and was quick to say he had it, but in actuality, the money had him! Even though he is sixteen like myself, he is a pretty smart kid, believe it or not. His father was brutally murdered when he was just six years old. His mother is a single woman who works at the hospital as a CNA. Her name is Ms. Jackson. She claims she has control of Pain, but sad to say, the streets have him now. That's my boy though; I love him to death. I just wish I had a legal business idea to present to him that would yield the same profits. Until then, my two cents don't matter pertaining to how another man provides for his family.

In addition to street fame, Pain has it made in a sense. He gets all the money and has White Boy Al doing his homework. He pays him in marijuana. On paper, he is as smart as me. I have a 4.0 and he is close behind with a 3.7. White Boy Al grew up on the hill with us. His parents were lawyers who divorced when he was young. His father raises him and he visits his mom in the summer in Colorado. He is an honorary member of the family, but we will never allow him to say "nigger!"

Even though we live in a rough town, The Hill is the best classroom. We learn the art of negotiation, detecting discernment, and survival skills to use as a GPS, to guide us through this matrix called life. I want to get a part-time job and help out with bills but I rarely have time. My parents want me to focus only on basketball because I am going into my junior year. I have to work on my game if I have any hope of being scouted and going D1. Everyone wants me to attend Duke University, but I have my eyes on Clark Atlanta University. They have one of the best business programs in the nation. On top of that, I will learn more about the history of our culture and get to meet some beautiful ladies from Spelman. I probably wouldn't even make it over there. The ratio at CAU is about 24 to 1! That's an easy decision for me to make. Don't you think?

It's November, and it is freezing in Jersey. Black ice paves the road and snow is the new grass. I had a game yesterday against Millville. I dropped thirty-two points and hit the game-winner from a long range. The video of me dunking on a fast break went viral. I received 200 new followers overnight and a few DM's from random women. I'm single. I know that's the devil trying to cash in on my talent though. The devil always sends a woman to knock you off your game from what I hear.

These Crackers are trying to cash in as well. They come to the hood with their metaphorical shopping cart and shop for the next best athletes to manage. The white man managing and the black man entertaining is always how it goes in this capitalistic system they've created. They have the money and we have the talent, the perfect love affair. The irony.

This knowledge I have comes from experience. I've seen it over and over. My cousin Bone went to the NBA and played for 3 seasons. The New York Knicks drafted Bone in the second round, but he barely made any money. The reason was due to him having to pay back advancements to his agents and other fees, which he had no knowledge of. He no longer has a dime of the money from the league. He is the janitor at Bridgeton High School now. He accepted his fate and he mentors me on and off of the court since everyone thinks I am next around here to be in the NBA. Bone stresses education to me and reminds me daily that "one day that ball will stop bouncing" and that I will have to figure out a way to survive after basketball.

That is one of the reasons why I read so much. So far, my favorite book is *26 Miles* written by this cat who uses the pen name Brother Brown. He is from Bridgeton but moved away after high school. He throws an annual "Stop The Violence" Basketball Tournament at the park each year. I met him last year at the tournament and he signed the book I purchased from him. He is one of my favorite authors. His writing style is very easy to understand. Other than his book my library consists of books such as:

How to Hustle and Win by Supreme Understanding
The Way of the Superior Man by David Deirda
Makes Me Want to Holler by Nathan McCall
Nigger by Dick Gregory
Art of War by Sun Zhu

Whoreson by Donald Goines
The Alchemist by Paulo Coelho
Revolutionary Suicide by Huey P Newton.

A book will take the mind places that the mind could not fathom.
If you can see it in your mind, then it can come to fruition. Believe
that!

Chapter 2:
LOYALTY IS EVERYTHING

Loyalty is the foundation that holds the strongest bonds together. It is impossible to build a house on a cloud. Without loyalty, nothing promising will ever come to those who break this sacred code.

-Brother Brown

I'm wolfing. I need to get a haircut before my next game so I can look good running up and down the court. I hear some scouts are going to be present. We play Vineland and that is our local rival being that it's only a mere two towns over. They have a few good players but I know they can't beat us. I'm going to score forty points and make a statement that Bridgeton is the best team in the county.

I reach in my pocket and find an old $20 bill. It's probably money I've left in the washing machine that survived the dryer. I'm glad it didn't rip! I can use this to pay for my haircut. I like to get my haircut at Wiz's Barbershop. Wiz is the owner. He only cuts part-time. He has many legit hustles to keep him busy. Every time I enter the barbershop he is always debating about various topics. I don't judge him though; I just soak up all the information and knowledge I can while he is here.

Before I even enter the shop, I hear his loud voice from outside in the middle of a debate. I am sure he is debating Nate, one of the other barbers who love to debate as well.

I enter.

"So you're telling me that African people weren't already in America when the slave ships landed?" Wiz asked Nate.

"America was great, and it was fully functioning due to all the Indian tribes and the civilizations they created," answers Nate.

"So what is the difference between an Indian and an African? Riddle me that genius?" asks Wiz.

"Listen, Wiz, there is no difference. They are both members of the same race."

"And what race is that?" Wiz asks as he rubs his chin hair.

"The human race, you dummy. The white man has you believing that we are separated in all these different categories. Ask Knowledge, he will confirm this."

"The human race is the only race we should attest to. All else is obsolete. The system has us divided, so they can easily conquer us. We are playing right into their system. We have to unite and fight." I say with confidence.

Wiz's face reads defeat. He took a deep breath and stood silent for a moment. Then he started laughing and stated,

"Nate you got me today, but tomorrow it is on. I will have my revenge. Thanks for the history lesson. Steel sharpens steel, you know I don't mind being corrected."

They dap each other up and head back to their stations. I flopped in Wiz's chair and told him to take me down a little and fade out my sides. He blows hair off his clippers and proceeds to cut my hair.

"How are you doing, Knowledge? By the way good game the other night, you had me scared for a minute. I was shaking in my boots."

"I apologize. My jumper was off. I tweaked my elbow in the first quarter. I'll be good by the time we play Vineland on Wednesday, though."

Bet, says Wiz as he pauses and stares at me. He is gazing at my hairline making sure it is even and sharp.

"Knowledge, you are the next messiah. You will rise to the top of the hill and help many people. The hood has your back, we are rooting for you."

I nod to let him know he is acknowledged.

Five minutes pass.

Pain walks in the barbershop and greets all the patrons. He sits down and begins to scroll on his phone.

"Ayo Pain, Wiz says I am the next messiah to lead the people. What you think, bro?"

"You already have my vote, Mr. President! You are the next Obama! You are the rose that grew from the concrete that Tupac referenced in his poems. You are a King, and I'm here to protect you from evil. I'll lay a man down for you. I'm loyal till they return me to the soil I was made in, kid."

Pain is loyal to me. I take nothing at face value, so before I confirmed his loyalty, I had to test it. Both of us have been pinned against each other with loyalty on the line. Some detectives were investigating Pain a few months ago. They interviewed me and tried to pin me on conspiracy charges because I was always with him. I survived the scare tactic. He beat the case easily and even sued the precinct for harassment. He won $100,000 but can't touch the money until he turns eighteen years old.

Why am I loyal to Pain you may be wondering? That's a great question.

I set Pain up to get kidnapped by my cousins from Philly. They snatched him and threw him inside a van and took him to an abandoned house. I had them keep his head covered until they got into the living room. I instructed them to show him a picture of me.

"Do you know Knowledge? He is the smart kid from the hill."

"Yeah, that's my man, what the fuck y'all want with him?"

"We need him off the streets waking up the people. These are orders strictly from the powers that be," says one of my cousins.

Pain asks breathing heavily, "What does that have to do with me?"

"We need you to kill him. Only you can get close enough. Kill him or we will kill you! So what is it going to be Pain?"

"All right I'll do it! How do you want me to do it?" Pain asks

"I want you to shoot him. Here is the gun. It's clean and after you do the job bring back my shit so I can dispose of it properly."

Pain takes the gun, tucks it, and says; "I'll see you soon."

As he exited towards the door he quickly reached for the weapon. He quickly turned around with his finger already on the trigger.

"Fuck all of you, I would rather die before I dishonor Knowledge."

BOOM! BOOM!
BOOM! BOOM!
BOOM! BOOM!

In the span of five seconds, Pain shot all three of my cousins twice. He then reached for the door but I was on the other side of it holding back with all my might. As he turned around towards my cousins they started laughing loudly. Pain, with the gun in hand, was looking distraught and very confused.

"What the fuck! I just shot y'all motherfuckers. How are y'all still alive?"

I rushed in the door laughing.

"Calm down Pain. This was staged, bro. Chill out."

"Knowledge what the fuck is going on bro? These fools just tried to get me to kill you kid. Why are you even here? What the fuck is so funny?" Pain asks, still looking confused.

"This was a loyalty test and you passed with flying colors bredren," I say to Pain in a Jamaican accent. "I'm getting out of the hood, and I am taking you with me!"

"As you should motherfucker, I told you I am with you. You thought I was playing? I wasn't," says Pain breathing hard while dusting himself off.

That is why we are indebted to each other. We want to see one another win at all times and at any cost. We are just going about it in two different ways. I'm using education and sports. Pain is using you know, the street game.

I pay Wiz with the crusty wrinkled twenty-dollar bill and head for the exit. As I leave the barbershop I tell everyone I love them, and that I will see them at the game on Wednesday. I was raised to always leave a conversation with love because life is short you know. You never know if the last time you speak to a person will be the last time. So if it is, what's more satisfying than knowing you told that person that you loved them as your final words?

Chapter 3:
GAME ALWAYS KNOWS GAME

There is nothing new under the sun. The schemes and scams are the same. The experience is the only thing that varies from person to person. Take heed to the wisdom of the elders.

-Brother Brown

As soon as I step outside the barbershop, whom do I run into? I ran into my cousin Jersey. He is always trying to sell the weirdest things at the weirdest times.

"Ayo cousin, how are you doing? Aye, check this out; I got these turtles for sale! I sell them for $20 but for you, give me $10," says Jersey in a smooth voice.

"Cuz, it's the middle of the winter, what the fuck am I gone' do with a damn turtle, huh? I should call animal control on your ass, and say you are selling illegal turtles smuggled from Somalia."

"Chill son, don't do that to me, baby. Remember, safety first cuz, make sure you play to win out here."

I dap him up and walk off. I'm hungry and I have spaghetti on my mind. I saved some leftovers from yesterday's dinner. I am going to devour that spaghetti as soon as I get home.

I walk home as fast as I can. Upon entering my building I run into the last person I want to see at this time of night. It's Peewee, the neighborhood fiend who is always panhandling and raising money for the weirdest causes.

The time is 7 pm.

"Yo Knowledge, what's up baby? Look I need $5 to get my dog back from the pawnshop. I pawned him to pay my phone bill in order for my mother to stay in touch in case of emergencies. Look out for me man, I'll wash your car tomorrow!"

"Not today Peewee, I don't have time for your shenanigans."

Peewee doesn't even have a dog, and plus his mother passed

away last month. He uses her death to play on the emotions of the victims he attempts to con. I'm hip to his games though. I bet you he will try me with the same story tomorrow. I just realized that he said he would wash a car that I didn't even have. He is one of the best panhandlers I know.

Let me tell you what he did one time. This fool is a genius. He went and put some Halloween makeup on from the dollar store and made it seem as if he had a gash on his head. It looked real; he even fooled me for a moment. His scam speech was he needed to go to the hospital but didn't have money for the co-pay fee. Peewee made almost $2,000 that day and bought pizza for the entire building.

Peewee always says, "I hope the people never wake up! There is a lucrative market for the sleeping sheep. I'm here to cash in on it, and enjoy my slice of the pie I've been deprived of my whole life."

He has a valid point, get it how you live I guess. There is nothing new under the sun. The schemes and scams are the same. The experience and results are the only things that vary. Take heed to the wisdom of the elders.

Peewee usually has this girl he gets high with, Roxanne, with him. She is about crazy as he is. She comes around and kicks it with us sometimes. I remember this one time, Peewee told us the "Junkie's Love Oath." He and Roxanne pledged allegiance to it together. It is what binds their souls. It reads as such:

If I ever OD,
I want you to follow right behind me
I want you to OD right beside me

I want you to hold me while I'm smiling
while I'm dying
And if you really know me
When I go missing,
You know where to find me

Meet me there.

I guess everyone has something they pledge allegiance to. I guess the goal of the user is to get high and die with the one you love. I don't know. Wait, I just noticed the *Junkies Love Oath* is a verse from The Weeknd off a song titled *Faith.* I told you he was the illest. Did he get you too? It's a legit song. Look it up.

I hop on the elevator and press two. I could have used the stairs but too much goes on there. Pain already laced me with the game. One time I took the stairs and seen Peewee having sex and shooting up heroin at the same time. As I walked past in disgust and turned the corner it got worse. I saw a woman was giving a blowjob to a dealer who lives in my building. She was sucking him while simultaneously holding her newborn baby. Ever since that day, I've been using the elevator. That was enough trauma for me. I exit the elevator and head to my apartment. I grab my key from my backpack and enter. I greet my parents and then head to my room. I toss my tethered backpack on my bed and head back to the kitchen. My mother notices my haircut and fake flirts with me.

"Can I have your number, handsome?"

"Yes, it's 281-330-8004, ask for Mike Jones," I respond sarcastically.

"My son has that good hair just like his daddy!" my pops chimes in.

"What good hair? You are bald, baby! Your head is about as smooth as my...oh, never mind", says my mother.

I laugh as I head to open the fridge. A full bowl of spaghetti awaits me. I love cheese. I grab a slice of yellow Kraft cheese and mix it into the spaghetti. After that, I placed the bowl in the microwave for two minutes. Thirty seconds later I hear a loud popping coming from the microwave. It sounded like WWIII in there! After two minutes, I take the bowl out. My spaghetti was still cold. I hate it when that happens. I placed the spaghetti back inside for a minute and a half. Then I proceeded to pour myself a cold glass of apple juice.

Ding!

The microwave rings its alarm and the kitchen smells heavenly. I grab the bowl and head to the table and turn on ESPN. The spaghetti is amazing. Sometimes leftovers are better than the real meal if you ask me. After I devoured the spaghetti I placed the dishes in the sink and headed to the bathroom to shower. I have school in the morning and practice in the afternoon. We have to win 5 of 6 remaining games if we are going to make the playoffs this year. I'm sure we can achieve that goal.

Chapter 4:
SPEAK YOUR MIND

Most respected individuals are not liked, and most liked people aren't respected. In the race of life, respect is the marathon, and being liked is the sprint. What race are you running?

-Brother Brown

I fell asleep exactly ten minutes after lying on my bed after that shower. My alarm wakes me daily at 5:45 am. Oh shit, I left the lamp on all night! Mom is going to kill me when she sees next month's light bill. No time to worry about that now, I have to get dressed. We wear uniforms at Bridgeton High School. They are strict with the dress code and quick to seize all opportunities to swag out our uniforms, with our individual flavors. I think they are preparing us for prison in a weird way. I will elaborate on that statement in a minute. I hear the news playing on the television in the kitchen. I head to the bathroom to conduct personal hygiene.

"Make sure you bundle up today, it's going to be 37 degrees," says the weatherman named Jeff Daniels.

After I brush my teeth, I head to my room to get dressed. I throw on my black khaki pants with my gray polo. Since today is supposed to be cold, I throw on my black Timberlands, my big red coat, and a black hat. I grab my backpack and turn off all the lights as I head for the kitchen.

"Good morning," I yawned to my parents.

"You are running late, I made you a sandwich to go", says my mother.

"Have a good day at school son, and lead with the truth at all times," says my pop.

A knock comes from the door. That must be Pain making sure I am up so we could walk to school together. It is Pain. I open the door and we shake hands. I wave to my parents while simultaneously locking the door on my way out.

"What's up with you bro?" I ask Pain as I dap him up again.

"Chilling, you heard what happened to Peewee?

"No, what did his crazy ass do now?"

"He overdosed last night, I found him and had to call the ambulance for his ass."

I know Pain was withholding some details. I look at him. I scold him with a face that reads discernment. He notices me catch on to his bullshit and starts laughing.

"Alright, you got me, bro. This is what happened. I gave him a sample of this new shit I just got in. Shit was too pure for him. Peewee hit it twice and started tweaking. I panicked and dragged his ass outside to the playground. I didn't want to bring attention to the spot you know. His ass is good though, he will probably be out of the hospital by the time school is out," explains Pain.

"Cut that shit when you get a chance. Overdosing addicts is bad for business"

I am no stranger to the game. I know the ins and outs of the urban underworld. My philosophy is that drugs are killing off our soldiers; soldiers that we need on the frontline when it's time for the revolution. With drugs plaguing the community we are bound to have a bunch of zombies on the frontline when it's time for war. If you live in the hood long enough, you will innately learn the language of the game automatically.

I walk in silence as we stroll to school. I felt sorry for Peewee. Even though Peewee is an addict, he is essential to the community. He is a vital member. He has a beautiful soul, but he just likes to get high. We all have our vices. They make us who we are.

We make it to school. The heat felt so good as it came into contact with my skin. I took off my hat and placed it in my bag. Pain and I headed to our homeroom and waited to hear today's news on the loudspeaker. White Boy Al walks in and hands Pain a vanilla folder on the slide. I'm sure that the folder contains the ten page persuasive essay due today. Pain tells Al he will take care of him later.

The school day goes by oddly fast, and now I am at my locker about to get my shoes for practice. Pain walks up and asks if everything is good. I nod. Al walks up. Thick ass Brianna walks by and calls us the three stooges. We snicker in unison and I tell her, "Be safe."

Pain thanked Al for his A on his chemistry test. He told him he has another essay due Friday. The topic was slavery. I told Pain with that specific topic he could knock out that easily himself and save some money.

"Knowledge, I don't know anything about no fucking slavery bro. Those particular events happened years ago my boy. I am free now. I can do whatever I want."

White boy Al chimes in and says, "Chill Knowledge, you are acting like you were a slave or something?"

"Yeah, when were you ever a slave, huh?" Pain adds with sarcasm in his tone.

I lost it at that point. I flashback momentarily to this morning and I hear my father telling me to lead with the truth at all times. I let them have it.

"I am a slave right now! I am a slave to this education system that

I am too smart for. But I have to go through this system so I can do my own thing one day. You know what else? Y'all two are slaves too! Pain, you are a slave and don't even know it. You are a slave to the money and them bitches you fuck with; they will be your downfall. Open your eyes! White boy Al, you are a slave to that weed. It controls your actions and keeps you in a daze. Done fuck up that white privilege bad you were born with. I'm on your ass, and you better wise up. You know what, fuck yall. I'm gone! I'll see y'all later; I'm going to practice."

I walk away and head for the gymnasium. By this time, a crowd formed around us making it seem like a fight was occurring. I hear the keys jingling as Mr. Davis sprints towards the scene of the altercation. When he arrives he shoves his way through the crowd.

"What's going on here? What is the problem?"

"Nothing Mr. Davis, we just arguing about slavery and how Knowledge thinks we are currently slaves."

Mr. Davis calls me back to the scene at my locker. I walk back as slow as I can. Upon my arrival, I am still high off logic and not emotion. My thoughts are sharp still. I let Mr. Davis' ass have it.

"Mr. Davis, you are a slave as well! The only thing that has changed is 'the cotton.' We are your cotton now. You are picking us! Picking us to be the newest victims of the wicked pipeline to prison. Is that why you're always so quick to call the police after every fight? You only see us as bad, problematic kids. We are humans, you know, and we are the future carriers of the baton. If you can't respect that, then I suggest you go back to policing the streets and harassing criminals, rather than provoking students who are trying to learn their way to a better life. Let me tell you something about respect. You have to give it to get it. Most respected individuals are not liked and most liked people aren't respected. In the race of life, respect is the marathon, and being like is the sprint. The marathon continues. Still, I run, Mr. Davis, still I run!"

Mr. Davis stood there puzzled for a minute. A hush fell over the crowd after my rant was over. Most of the things I said went over the heads of everyone present. I check my locker to ensure it is locked, and walk off and head to the gymnasium.

Pain and White Boy Al start to converse.

"Knowledge is always on that black power shit," mumbles White Boy Al.

"He isn't saying anything wrong, we are just playing the cards we were dealt," replies Pain.

"I guess, but I will have that paper completed and to you by Thursday," says Al.

"Bet, and here is an ounce of the best bud in the city for your hard work. I'll catch you later kid, I have a few runs to make," says Pain as he walks away.

He quickly turns around and hands Al an ounce of weed, and says he is paying him in advance. Al tucks it and walks off nonchalantly.

See that's the problem with people. They don't want to change. They see no wrong in their actions. You can drop all the jewels on them, and give them 'all the free game' but to no avail. People are going to be people. Let them.

On my way to the gymnasium, I ran into Sue. She is the most beautiful senior to ever walk the halls of BHS. I greet her with a hug and soft kiss on the cheek. She pushes me off and tells me to watch it.

"You can't handle me Knowledge, don't bite off more than you can chew."

"Listen I always score when I shoot my shot, I haven't air-balled since the 5th grade, baby. I'll see you at the game on Wednesday. I am bringing the state championship to the Bridge for the first time in years!"

She smirks and blushes as I walk off. My confidence makes me attractive to older women. I guess it's just what comes with the game. I enter the locker room to change my clothes. I am fifteen minutes early so I have time to chill for a minute. Big Man walks in to change for practice as well. His real name is Theodore Bartholomew Jenkins, but that shit is too long for us to say. He is 6 foot 7 so we just call him "Big Man." I tie up my Jordan 12's and head for the court. I see coach Sco standing in the middle of the court. He is a baldheaded, cool, smooth guy who always drops jewels on us before practice to keep us sane. He is from the town as well, so it is safe to say he knows a thing or three.

"Life is a marathon, a series of ups and down on a quest towards a particular goal. I pray for each and every one of you. I hope you all learn from the mistakes of others and use that energy as fuel to escape this place. With that being said, let me get twenty laps," says Coach in the middle of the huddle.

Coach Sco is all about conditioning. He will never let us lose a game due to conditioning. I feel like we run 26 miles a week, but I can see it paying off. I rarely get tired during games. There is a method to his madness. To understand you just have to simply buy into his system. After the completion of the laps, we stretch and run our new plays. We have this one play called "Overload" which is a play to get me open for a backdoor alley-oop. That's my favorite of the four new plays we have. We are going to make the playoffs. I can feel it. The team is focused and we have something to prove. After practice, Coach tells us that practice is canceled tomorrow due to him having to attend a funeral. He tells us that the gym would be open if we want to come to shoot around. We play Vineland on Wednesday. He tells us to be ready.

"This game will either make us or break us in our playoff run."

We all nod in unison and I tell Coach that we accept the challenge and we won't let him down.

"All right, bring it in," I instruct my teammates.

"DOGS FOR LIFE ON 3!" I say loudly in the middle of the huddle.

"1,2,3 DOGS FOR LIFE!" we say in unison as we head back to the
          locker room.

Chapter 5:
GOD VS. THE DEVIL

There is a constant war for the souls of mortal men. They say the urban environment is the devil's playground. The devil pumps hate, envy, and jealousy into the atmosphere, while simultaneously God pumps love, trust, and unity into it. This spiritual war has been going on since the beginning of time. The only result of war is death. Some of us are alive but still mentally dead. We have nothing to live for or to look forward to. That is why it is so easy to become employed by the devil and do his dirty work. Steer clear from these people at all costs!

-Brother Brown

I get dressed and leave out the locker room. Before I make it out the parking lot, a black jeep pulls up on me. The window rolls down slowly. My heart drops because I don't recognize the car.

Is this my demise? I pull out my gold knife just in case.

"Get in bro, hurry up. Put that little ass knife away before you cut yourself!" yells Pain from the backseat.

I jump in without hesitation and place my knife back in my pocket.

"What's up, bro? Everything good?"

"Jersey just got shot, kid! They tried to rob him. He was on the Southside selling designer bags and boots when it occurred" says Pain.

"Is he okay? Where is he now? Is he going to make it?"

A single tear races from my eye to my chin. I sniffle a few times. My heart is pounding. I just saw him yesterday with them damn turtles. Why would someone want to shoot him?

"It was the young boys from the north side. I don't want to start a war with Money and his crew but I will. I have my wolves out lurking as we speak. Jersey is like a brother to me. I will handle this, I just came to make sure you were good, and make sure you get home safe."

"Thanks, bro, I appreciate you," I say to him as we skirt off in the black jeep.

As we approach my building everyone is stopping me to explain theories about what they think happened to my cousin Jersey.

Nas said it best on "Represent,"

Straight up shit is real
Any day could be your last in the jungle
Get murdered on the humble
*Guns blast, and n****s tumble*

Shootings have become the norm around here. It was written I guess. Now everyone is shouting out information and spreading false rumors.

"Sorry about your cousin, he was just fucking with the wrong people."

"He was just in the wrong place at the wrong time."

"I heard it was them young boys from the north side that robbed him."

The atmosphere is toxic and flooded with a multitude of frequencies. Misery loves company and everyone is using this situation as a scapegoat from their personal problems. I look up and see people watching from their windows being nosey. This is one of the problems I have with the hood, people don't know how to support and show love without the drama.

There is a constant war for the souls of the mortal men. They say the urban environment is the devil's playground. The devil pumps hate, envy, and jealousy into the atmosphere, while simultaneously God pumps love, trust, and unity into it. This spiritual war has been going on since the beginning of time. The only result of war is death. Some of us are alive but still mentally dead. We have nothing to live for or to look forward to. That is why it is so easy to become employed by the devil and do his dirty work. Steer clear from these people at all costs! It will cost you in the long run.

Looking past the crowd, I notice my father walking up. I'm sure he is about to diffuse the situation. He was wearing all black pants, black boots, and a black leather jacket. He was in panther mode. I knew he was about to drop some knowledge. I like to see pops in this rare form. I'm sure these types of altercations occurred often when he was running with the Black Panthers.

My father enters the crowd and heads for the center. With a deep raspy voice that demands respect, my father began his message. The crowd circles around all while continuing talking loud and acting like savages.

"ALL RIGHT LISTEN UP!"

"Man shut the fuck up Mr. T! We ain't trying to hear that black power shit tonight!" someone yells from the crowd.

"WHO SAID THAT? COME SAY IT TO MY FACE!" yells my father with fire in his eyes and smoke coming from the top of his head.

A hush fell over the crowd and nobody stepped up to claim the statement. My father started his speech:

"Violence and the Devil are first cousins. They have just knocked on the door of our community once again. We have to rid our community of the people who commit these senseless crimes against their own people. This crime hits home because it happened to someone who is dear to me. My own nephew: whom we all know as Jersey. I want you all to know he is going to pull through. I received the call a few minutes ago from the hospital."

Chapter 6:
KILL THE MESSENGER

The messenger must die. He is loyal only to the cause. He is on neither side. He sets the stage for war, then fades to black and enjoys the show. He mentally orgasms off of the demise of the humans he chooses to pin against one another. The thrill keeps him going. The messenger is the devil, and this move is one of his oldest tricks. So when people come to me with the "he said, she said" I never send a message back. I just say to myself, "we will bump shoulders eventually. This world is small enough"

-Brother Brown

Wednesday has finally come. As Pain and I enter the school and successfully make it through the metal detectors, the students let out battle cries and warrior chants. They are excited about tonight's game. I'm wearing my jersey on top of my gray polo shirt. I wear number eleven. There is no story behind my number selection. That is just the number I chose. As we stroll to breakfast I see Courtney from afar. She is the captain of the cheerleaders. I yell out her name to get her attention. I start walking faster towards her. As she slowly turns around I see two maroon number ones painted on her face. As I get closer I also notice a nicely detailed Bulldog logo painted on the right side of her forehead. Then I noticed her beauty. She was brown-skinned with a beautiful smile, and a natural Afro that was always greased to perfection. The scent of cocoa butter bombarded my nose hairs as I arrived at her destination. She was well-groomed and comes from a good home. I could sense it. She aspires to be a nurse one day, but she loves sports. She is big on research and quick to read me my stats.

"Good morning Courtney, You are in the school spirit I see," I yawn sarcastically as we embrace each other.

"Hell Yeah! We're going to' kick their ass tonight" she replies looking jittery and excited.

Mr. Davis walks up and tells Courtney to watch her mouth, and quickly walks off.

Pain still standing there adds his two cents,

"I'll let you two lovebirds have it. Knowledge, what do you want from the café? I'll bring it to homeroom for you."

"Bring me a cinnamon bagel, regular cream cheese, and an orange juice. And for Courtney, get her an apple."

I spoke too soon. She reached in her coat pocket and revealed a green apple she stated thanks but no thanks. She had her own breakfast.

I dap up Pain, then he heads for the cafeteria. Courtney and I start down the hallway to our respected homerooms. She pulled out a wrinkled paper and started hitting me with my stats. It is too early for this but criticism is what I need to accept in order to know what to work on. That is the only way to become a better player. Courtney doesn't bite her tongue for anything. She speaks her mind at all times.

"You had thirty-two points last game, but shot terribly. You went 13 for 30 from the field. You stunk it up! Those stats mean you shot a low percentage of 43%. Now your season average shooting percentage is down to 72%. Pass the ball some more as well. Utilize the big man when your shot is not falling. Last game you did the total opposite. You just kept shooting. So my advice for tonight is to feed Theodore more. By doing that, the opponents will double him and that will get you open for better quality shots. Oh yeah, I want to let you know that Clark Atlanta University and Duke University scouts will be present tonight. Play your game and you will be okay. Thanks for walking me to my homeroom, see you tonight. Good luck again!"

"Thanks, Coach!" I say sarcastically as I walk off.

She made a lot of sense though. I will apply her logic on the court tonight.

I enter the classroom and I see Pain already present. He must've cut through B Hall. That's the only way he would beat me here. He hands me the bag with all my requested items. To my surprise, the bagel is still warm. I break the bagel in half and I inhale the cinnamon scent. It makes me even hungrier. I grab the cold cream cheese packet and open it. As I begin to spread the topping on my bagel, I notice White Boy Al enters the classroom and heads towards Pain and I. I continue to spread this white greatness on this beautiful bagel.

"Why are you late White Boy Al?"

"I overslept, I was up late watching the game. LeBron James went off last night,"

Waiting for the next statement I take a bite into my cinnamon and cream cheese concoction. I tell Pain that we should go into the bagel business. He laughs it off and tells me to stick to basketball. White Boy Al says he has a message for me and hands me the newspaper.

Pain immediately snatches the newspaper and throws it. Al gets mad and pushes Pain and states he paid good money for that newspaper. The shove was pointless. Pain barely moved. I stand there trying to process what the hell went wrong so fast and why these two fools are interrupting my bagel time. I finish my bagel. My mouth was drier than desert sand. The orange juice was clutch in this situation. After a few gulps, I began to get to the bottom of what just occurred.

"Pain, what the fuck, bro? Why did you throw the paper? What did it say?"

"It was an article about tonight's game. Vineland is talking shit and Jamal Warner said he is shutting you down and dropping forty points in the doghouse tonight. I don't need any other frequencies running through your mind. I want you on the right channel at all times. I don't want you trying to make it a one on one game tonight just to prove a point. I knew he was talking trash. I didn't tell you because the messenger of any bad news must die!"

"Die? Why?" asks White Boy Al with a confused look on his face.

Pain explains. "Yes, he must die because the information that he is attempting to transmit could be detrimental. It is most of the time. See with that newspaper you were going to throw Knowledge off of his game tonight. Knowledge was going to sacrifice the game to prove a point to Jamal Warner. Let us not forget the mission of this season; WIN THE STATE CHAMPIONSHIP, not prove a point and entertain small things. Look at the bigger picture. Al, you should know better. I have big money on this game tonight and I am not taking any chances. This here is a thinking man game."

Mr. Brown, our homeroom teacher, overhears the conversation and asks Pain to explain why the messenger must die again. He only heard bits and pieces.

Pain takes a deep breath and elaborates on his statement. "This is why the messenger must die. He is loyal only to the cause. He is on neither side. He sets the stage for war, then fades to black and enjoys the show. He mentally orgasms off of the demise of the humans he chooses to pin against one another. The thrill keeps him going. The messenger is the devil, and this move is one of his oldest tricks. So when people come to me with a message like Al did to Knowledge or the regular "he said, she said" I never send a message back. I just say to myself, "we will bump shoulders eventually. This world is small enough. So tonight Knowledge and Jamal Warner will bump shoulders on the court and solve all differences there. In the streets, things would have been solved differently. Somebody would end up dead for 9 times out of 10: nothing."

Pain looks at Al and tells him again that he has to be careful of the messages he intends to convey to the group. Nothing can come between this thing of ours. Nothing!

Mr. Brown is intrigued by the morning philosophy session. He was surprised by the wisdom and wit of Pain.

"What books have you read that have shaped your thinking?" Mr. Brown asks Pain while he rubs his chin hairs.

"I read urban novels, but most of my game comes from experience. You have to live a little bit on the wild side, Mr. Brown, you know?" Pain replies in his philosophical voice.

Mr. Brown stood in silence and then headed back to his desk to do his daily attendance check.

I noticed an unfamiliar face in the class. It's a black dude who is staring at me. I get the attention of Pain to make him aware. We approach him and make our introduction.

"What's up, black man? They call me Pain and this is my boy, Knowledge. Who are you?

"What's up, G, They call me Curtis! I'm from Chicago G."

"You seem cool; if you need anything let me know. I run these halls."

"Bet that up, G."

"Is 'G' your favorite letter or something?" I ask

"Na G, you have to be from the Chi to understand. That is just how we talk. On 'foe nem'."

"What does that mean? On 'foe nem'? I ask with a confused face.

"You wouldn't understand that either, once again you have to be from Chicago to comprehend G."

"I get it. Your favorite letter is G and your favorite number is four or should I say foe. If you like it, I love it, my brother. You have a good day Curtis. By the way, welcome to Bridgeton High School."

I head to grab my backpack from the back of the classroom. The bell rings. It's time to head to my first-period class of the day. Gym. I toss my black gym bag in my maroon locker and head to the gymnasium. A few students hug me and tell me good luck tonight. Everyone seems excited about the game. I am cool, calm, and collected. I reach the gymnasium. I am pretty early. I stand in the middle of the court and close my eyes. I envision the packed house tonight as I zone out. I hear the crowd chanting my name. *KNOWLEDGE, KNOWLEDGE, KNOWLEDGE!*

Yeah, I can see them now.

I snap out of my daydream.

I notice we have a substitute. We will probably have a free day today. I change clothes in the gym locker room and head back out so I can be present for attendance. After the politics of roll call is over, I hear the basketballs roll out. Most of my classmates quickly start pickup games. I don't want to risk getting an injury so I take a

ball and go shoot free throws. Juan, my classmate, walks up. He is
a short Mexican who likes to talk about sports.

"Knowledge bro, is it cool if I like get your rebounds bro?" asks
Juan.

I grant his wishes while simultaneously asking myself "Why do
Mexicans say bro so much per sentence? The world may never
know."

I shot about two- hundred free throws in the forty-minute period.

Juan points to the bleachers.

"Knowledge bro, when you dunk tonight bro, point to me in the
crowd bro. I will appreciate you forever bro."

See what I mean? He said it four times in one sentence!

"I got you, bro," I say sarcastically.

Gym class will be over in ten minutes. Now it's time to get dressed
and get ready for the next class: Math. After I get back into
uniform, I make my way out of the gym and head to math class.
All those free throws burned all my energy. I am hungry again.

I reach math class and greet my teacher, Mrs. Jones. After roll call,
she starts to hand out last week's tests.

She stood in the center of the front of the class and bore us the
bad news.

"Listen, class, you all need to start taking your time with your
math problems. Some of you are rushing and it shows. These test

scores made my stomach turn."

My stomach dropped. I have to get an A. My GPA cannot suffer. I sit in the front row of the class. You can tell a lot about a student based on where they sit. Mrs. Jones placed the test on my desk face down. I turned it over as quickly as I could. A+ circled in red ink with a smiley face. I laugh to myself and place the test in my bag. For the remainder of class, Mrs. Jones had me help other students with their tests. She gave them partial credit for them explaining where they went wrong on the test. The students appreciated her gesture. Mrs. Jones told us Christmas came early this year.

Forty minutes pass. The bell rings.

"Good Luck tonight Knowledge, my husband and I will be present at the game cheering you guys on" states Mrs. Jones

I thank her as I head towards the door.

The next period was History class. Mr. Hudson is the teacher for this course. On this particular day, I guess he didn't feel like teaching. He popped in a movie about Frederick Douglas and scrolled on his phone for the remainder of the class. The movie was interesting and I learned some new facts about Black History I wasn't aware of.

Another forty minutes fly by.

The bell rings again and now it is time for lunch. I jog to the cafeteria because I am starving at this point. I see Pain and Al at the table we always sit at. I walk up and take my seat. White Boy Al is beat boxing and Pain is nodding his head waiting to chime in. Pain spits a few bars. It was pretty dope.

AYO
THEY CALL ME PAIN YO
BECAUSE THAT'S ALL I BRING YO
ALL AROUND THE TOWN
MY NAME RING YO
SEE I GET MONEY
AND I GET ALL THE HONEYS
WHY YOU LAUGHING KNOWLEDGE?
NOTHING IS FUNNY
MY RHYME IS DONE
I'M TOO MUCH FOR YALL DUMMIES!
I'M OUT
SIKE!
AL KEEP THE BEAT GOING
SO I CAN KEEP FLOWING
THE MOTTO IS
RUN WITH US
OR GET RUN OVER
THE NAME IS PAIN
I'M GOING TO LIVE AND DIE
AS A COBRA
TSSSSSS...

"AYYYEEE!! That rap was dope, kid," I say to him as I dap him up.

"Now it's your turn, kid," he says as he calls everyone to the table.

Now the table is crowded and Al still has the beat going.

"GO KNOWLEDGE, GO KNOWLEDGE", the students roar as they await my rap.

I don't know whether to start pop-locking or start rapping at this point. Even though I don't rap, here goes nothing.

"AYO
THEY CALL ME KNOWLEDGE
IN TWO MORE YEARS IM OUT OF HERE
I'M GOING TO COLLEGE
I WANT TO GIVE A SHOUTOUT TO MY FATHER
HE RAISED ME RIGHT
I LIVE A HELL OF A LIFE
AND FUCK JAMAL WARNER
VINELAND IS GOING DOWN TONIGHT"
HE CAN'T GUARD ME
NOBODY CAN
I'M THE MAN
TONIGHT I'M GOING FOR 40
AFTER I DUNK
I'M GOING TO BLOW A KISS AT HIS SHORTY
BULLDOG FOR LIFE

Everyone goes crazy at the table. I hi-five everyone and hug a few of the girls that were present. This is a golden moment. This moment has to be captured. I pull out my phone and tell everyone to get in for a picture. I extend my arm as high as it can go and take the shot. This picture will be worth more than a thousand words.

"Send that to me, kid," instructs Pain

My table is called up to get our lunch. My stomach growls as I wait in line. I see the menu. It reads "Cheesesteaks and French fries" which is my favorite meal. I grab the cheesesteak and a Gatorade and make my way back to the table. As I walk back I see Big Man. We nod simultaneously. I'm sure he has been getting told good luck all day as well. I devour my lunch quickly. I don't know why I eat so fast. The school day is almost over. I just have to get through a few more classes, Science and English.

Chapter 7
GAME TIME

In the face of adversity is where man's true character is born. He can rise to the occasion or he can fold like origami. A man doesn't make excuses. He finds a way or he makes one!

-Brother Brown

The time has come. Game time is in thirty minutes. Loud whistles blow as the crowds cheer, and the coaches yell. The junior varsity team is playing. The score is 45-56 with five minutes remaining in the 4th quarter. They are losing. Looking in the stands, I notice Sue and wave at her. She waves back. Glancing to the other side of the bleachers sits Jamal Warner. He is listening to music via headphones. He notices me looking his way. We locked eyes. Warner wore a stoic expression, but I could care less. I'm from the hill, Cobra territory so he is going to have to come harder than that to intimidate me. He then insinuates him cutting off my head with a gesture. While smirking and laughing, I nod my head up and down. I got something for him. He is in for a special treat tonight.

Courtney saw the whole scene.

She came out of the blue and crept up on me.

"Stay focused on the game. Don't let him get into your head. Remember what I told you this morning. Use your teammates to your advantage. Good luck!"

I hug her then head back into the locker room to get dressed.

My shoes for tonight are my custom Jordan 12's. They are maroon and white. I throw on my black compression shorts, then my team shorts. I throw my jersey over my head and pull it down. It is time. I head to the bathroom. I look in the mirror and mean mug my reflection. I hear coach Sco walk in. He instructs us to bring it in. It is time for his pre-game speech.

"Listen up fellas, tonight is a big game. We have to make a statement that we are serious. This game will be full of ups and downs. Keep your heads up out there. Keep your composure and don't get rattled. Now bow your heads. Let us pray."

We bow our heads and hold hands.

"Dear Lord, we come to you with humble hearts and open minds. Thank you for allowing us to play yet another game; we ask that you cover us and keep us safe during this battle we are about to endure. Let us not be afraid in the face of adversity. Let us all rise to the occasion and conquer our enemies. Thanks in advance for the future blessings you plan to bestow upon us. Amen!"

We say "Amen" in unison.

I take control of the situation.

"Y'all know what we have to do. Let's protect our house. Bring it in. DOGS FOR LIFE ON THREE, ONE TWO THREE."

"DOGS FOR LIFE!!!"

Coach hands me a basketball. We line up at the door. I peek out into the gym from the locker room door. The gym is packed to capacity! The cheerleaders are lined up shaking their pom-poms and cheering. Lights flash as the crowd awaits our entrance onto the court to start our warm-ups. The JV game ends. Vineland runs out and our crowd boos them excessively. I keep the door open so I can hear the queue to come out.

It is game time.

"Let's go dogs", I say as I look back to see if they were ready.

They were! I opened the door and led my troops through the barrage of pompoms and screaming fans. Nipsey Hussle's song

"Last Time That I Checked" played as we ran out. I can't lie; the whole build-up to the game is my favorite part.

Pain hands me a piece of gum and we do our custom handshake. He is sitting with the cobras. I chew the winter fresh gum as I wait my turn in the layup line. I'm up. I grab the ball and finger roll it into the basket. I could have dunked it, but I'll save that for the game. I notice my parents enter the gym. I hug my mother and shake hands with my father. I love to see them in the stands. It makes me feel whole. I look up and we have two minutes left to shoot around.

As I shoot around and stretch, I notice Pain walk over to the bleachers where the Vineland fans were congregating. Pain must be looking to finesse a bet on tonight's game. He starts talking junk to the fans accompanied by the cobras.

"Fuck all this talking who wants to bet on the game? Put your money where your mouth is. I have $5000 that the bulldogs win tonight. Going once, going twice." asks Pain with a huge wad of cash in his hands.

"Make it ten! Jamal Warner is about to show out tonight. I have $10,000 I am willing to bet. So what's it going to be?" asks Julio who is the leader of the Rican Posse.

The "Rican Posse" is known to get busy in the streets, but Pain and Julio have mutual respect for one another. Less violence means more money for both parties.

"It's a bet! I will be here at the end of the game to collect. Don't try anything dumb, you won't make it to your car." says Pain as he walks back to his original seat with the cobras.

While all that was going on, Coach Sco called us over to the bench. I sit on the bench along with the other starters. We wait for our introductions. Our crowd is booing every player that gets introduced from Vineland. Their show is over. They save me for the last to be introduced.

"A sophomore guard, six-foot phenomenon. Everybody get on your feet and make some noise for Dre Peters aka Knowledge!" says the announcer.

I run through the line and shake hands with their coach and get ready for the national anthem. Courtney sings it usually. She has a beautiful voice.

Okay, enough with the pre-game politics. Let's get to the tip-off.

Big Man lines up against Jamal Warner. The ref tosses it up and both giants leap to retrieve it. Jamal got the best of Big Man and tapped it to his guard. First play of the game they ran a double screen for Jamal Warner. He ended up wide open in the corner for a three-pointer. Swish! I bring the ball up and Warner steals it from me. I fall trying to chase him down as he goes in for a wide-open dunk. Damn we down 5-0 that fast. As the quarter continues I am stinking it up on the court. Jamal Warner is dominating. He hasn't missed a three-pointer yet.

The first quarter ends. The scoreboard reads 20-8. We are down twelve. So far I am 0-5 from the field. Only scored two points, which were free throws. In the huddle, the coach is screaming and hollering at us.

"Y'all don't want to play today, or something? Let me know now because I will just end the game here. You guys are pissing me off! Keep your composure on the court. Their little storm is over. It is time to turn this thing around. Let's go Dogs!" says Coach Sco.

The second quarter starts and it seems as if everything the coach just said, went out the window. Big man can't make a lay-up for shit. I am passing the ball and everyone is playing scared. I glance in the crowd. Sue is pulling on her hair and shaking her head in frustration. I can feel her anger. My stock is dropping! The buzzer sounds off and it is now halftime. 35-20 is the score. Jamal Warner has 20 points.

Pain is livid and very upset. Directly across the gym, he hones in on Julio. He and his posse are dapping each other up. Julio, feeling himself, yells across the gym to Pain.

"This is easy money Pain, thanks in advance."

Pain flicked off Julio as he exited the bleachers.

We head to the locker room. Our heads are down. They took our hearts! Once in the locker room, my teammates and I start arguing and hollering about responsibilities.

Coach Sco walks in and throws his clipboard against the locker.

"I am speechless. You guys are playing like shit. This is not bulldog basketball!"

Pain walks into the locker room. Coach Sco jumps directly in his face. They lock eyes.

"Young man, you are not welcome here. This locker room is for players only. Now is not the time to be in here. This is my team, so that means my rules. I will kindly ask you to leave." says Coach Sco

"I respect your wishes coach, but I have a message for Knowledge. I think it will benefit the team. Just give me five minutes coach. Thank me later," pleads Pain

"You have three!"

Pain and I walk away from everyone. We head to the opposite side of the locker room.

"What's up with you bro? You are playing like shit tonight!" Who is the best player in the county?

"I am!"

"Who is the best player in Bridgeton?

"I am!"

Who is the best player on the court tonight?

"I am!"

"Man, I don't believe that shit. Show me better than you can tell me. This is your house. You need to protect it. You say you are the best, but currently, it's looking like Jamal Warner. Show me something in this second half. Tighten up, champ!"

In the face of adversity is where man's true character is born. He can rise to the occasion or he can fold like origami. A man doesn't make excuses. He finds a way or he makes one!

I head back towards my team. I tell them the second half is ours.

The third quarter starts and I am now guarding Jamal Warner. I decided to end his show and lock him down. I bring the ball up and yell out "Overload". Big Man comes to the top of the key and sets a huge pick. I pass to the wing and make a quick cut backdoor for the alley hoop. The lob was tipped, but the ball still made its way towards the rim. I jump up in an attempt to complete the dunk. So did Jamal Warner.

Boom!

I catch the alley hoop and slam it right on top of him. The crowd erupts as I point to Juan in the crowd. The refs call a foul and send me to the free-throw line. I am in my zone now. It is time for me to prove why I am the best on the court. I make the free throw and head back on defense. Warner comes down and tries to make a play. He ends up turning the ball over. He is doing too much. We have the ball now. I bring it up slowly and wave off Big Man. I call for isolation. I crossed over right and crossed over left. Warner bit. I pulled up for the wide-open three-pointer. Swish! I have my powers back.

Vineland calls a timeout.

In the huddle, the coach tells us to keep up the energy. He tells me to stay aggressive offensively and continue to harass Jamal Warner defensively. The time out ends and me and my platoon take the court to defend the doghouse. There are four minutes left in the third quarter. Warner and I are trading buckets and the crowd is enjoying the show. The third quarter ends and the score is now 50-42. We have won the battle but the war is far from over.

The 4th quarter starts. I bring the ball up and call for a pick. I go around it and head in for a layup. I get fouled and head to the line for two free throws. The first one drops.

"Aye Knowledge, I'm not convinced of what you told me at halftime. Show me something! Bring this shit home kid," yells Pain from the bleachers

I nod my head and tell him to watch this. The second free throw falls and I run back on defense. We are within six. Coach instructs us to press full court. Vineland wasn't expecting that. We got three steals in a row and tied the game up. Vineland called a timeout. We were all tied up at 50.

"Julio get my money ready!" yells Pain from the bleachers towards Julio

"Give me the ball, I will win this game for us. Follow my lead", I say to my team in the huddle.

There are three minutes left. I am nervous but I am not showing it. Jamal Warner comes down and pulls up for the three in my face. Swish! As he trots back on defense he places his pointer finger over his lips. The crowd boos him.

"Pain you better not be a dollar short!" yells Julio towards Pain

I get the ball and feed it to Big Man. He dunks and gets the foul. He makes the free throw and we have tied up once again at 53 a piece.

One minute remains.

Warner gets the ball and scores on a mid-range jumper. I have to admit, his 'game' is tough. He picks me up at half court and tells me this is his house now. That was the last straw. I call for isolation. Warner wipes the bottom of his shoes and gets in his defensive stance. I dribble through the legs twice. He was expecting me to drive. I cross him over and step back for the three. It goes on the net. Ten seconds remain. We are up one 56-55.

Vineland called their last timeout.

Coach tells me to stay on Warner and don't let him get an open shot. The refs blow their whistle and call us back onto the court. The whole gym is on its feet. We are in our full-court man defense. Warner gets the ball. He crosses over and I am now guarding him. He shoves me and I fall. Nothing was called. He continued up the court. He reached the three-point line and found an open seam.

"3,2,1" the crowd yells as he hoists up the jumper from long range.

We all stare and watch the ball head for the rim. It went in then bounced out. We won the game. My teammates lift me up and carry me off to the locker. I instructed them to let me down so I could tell Warner he had a good game.

I notice Pain approaching me. We embrace and he is satisfied with my performance.

"I see my halftime speech worked. Maybe I should be coaching you motherfuckers? Coach Sco ain't got shit on me kid. Just kidding but good game bro, I will see you later. I have to go collect my earnings. You gone' make me rich, kid. Keep it up!" says Pain as he walks off.

Pain approaches Julio to collect his winnings. Julio hands over the $10,000 peacefully and lets him know how he felt.

"Man, that was a good game. Jamal Warner had a chance to win it but he missed the shot. I lost the bet fair and square. You 'be safe' out here, bro. I'm out."

Julio and Pain dap each other up and both groups head for the exit.
Once in the locker room, we pour water over each other and hug one another. Coach walks in and shuts us down.

"Why are we celebrating? We haven't won anything yet! Next week we have Buena so keep that same energy. Get dressed I will see you all at practice tomorrow"

I get dressed and head outside. The gym is usually empty at this point. I walk out and I see Sue.

"You had me scared for most of the game, but you did what you do best. I want you to come over on Saturday. My parents are going out of town. Here is my number. Make sure you use it!"

I smile and make my way outside for my parent's car.

CHAPTER 8:
THE WAIT IS OVER

Patience is a superpower. It will keep you sane as you wait.

-Brother Brown

Time flew by after Sue gave me the green light to pull up. The thought of her has my mind clouded. I call her and let her know I am on the way. She lives about fifteen minutes away. I decide to walk and get some exercise. She tells me the door would be unlocked and to come straight upstairs. I arrive and do just that. The music was coming from the middle room. I figured she was behind it waiting for me. I twisted the knob and pushed the door forward.

Take You Down by Chris Brown plays in the background.

She was ready for me. I was ready for her. We wasted no time. She knew exactly what she wanted.

Sue lay on the bed stretched out. Body language read that she was comfortable. I am excited. All my blood rushed to my dick. I kid you not; I was harder than a roll of quarters. I reach for her waistline and begin to massage her upper thighs. She moans softly. She is wearing some black thin Nike tights and a crop top to match. I gently pull down the tights. I get them to her knees and look up. All I see is skin. Her panties are missing! I think I saw them on the back of a milk carton. She wiggles her hips to assist me in taking off her garments. Once off, I place them on the floor. She sits up and takes the crop top off. She asks if I can help her get out of her bra. I untangled the latch and she laid back. I can't believe I am about to have sex with her. I have been flirting with her for two years but to no avail. I stand up and take my clothes off.

"This bed has a 'no clothes' policy."

"Is that right?"

I pounced on her and gently kissed her twice as I stared deeply into her eyes. Her lips were so soft. I thought I was kissing two marshmallows for a minute. I made my way to the neck and went for what I know. I lick and kiss her neck slowly. She started rubbing my back softly. Then I turned it up a notch. I treated her neck like new flesh, and I was a zombie from the walking dead. She is shivering with excitement. She reaches for my dick and proceeds to insert it into her. I wiggle it into her warm portal of life. She exhales softly.

"This is what you've been waiting for. Come on and put your name on it."

Thinking to myself. Patience is really a superpower. It keeps a man sane as he waits patiently on things to manifest. Let me get back to the story.

From the first stroke, I knew I wasn't going to be in it long. I was too excited. I slowly stroked her and gently kissed her simultaneously. She starts to thrust me from under. She is about to end the show early. I try to think about basketball to get my mind off busting a nut. That shit didn't work. I feel the tingle building up, and my knees weaken. I pulled out and let it spray. This was my first time. I guess I was backed up because when I came, it shot all the way up to her nipples. She instructs me to go get a hot rag. I returned quickly and began to wipe my semen off her naked body.

"Sorry about that"

"Look at you looking all stupid, I knew you couldn't handle me. I told you so!"

She gets dressed and we head to the living room and watch TV. Martin was on. I watch silently because I am still upset I went out like a sucker. She notices my emotional shift and laces me with some motivation.

"Listen, Knowledge, I like you. You are different. I like your mind and the way you think. My feelings for you are more than just sex. By the way, I came twice in those thirty seconds so don't feel bad. You will get better with practice. The next time I have the house to myself, we can try again. Maybe then, you will last long enough to hit it from the back."

My lips curve up and a smile is born. I couldn't even hold it back. I like Sue too. She has a beautiful soul. She checks the time and lets me know that I have to go soon. Her parents are coming back. I head to her room and put my clothes back on. My spirit meter is green. I just hit the most beautiful girl in the school. No one can tell me shit right now. Wait until Pain hears about this.

"So, like am I your girlfriend now?" asks Sue.

"Listen, Sue, no you are not my girl. I like you or whatever but a relationship is not on my radar at this point in my life. I have a lot on my plate with sports and school. You would slow me down. I have big goals I plan to reach in life. Until I reach them everything is on the back burner. I am just being honest. Also, you women are too careful for my liking. All you know is school, work, and home. I hate that routine, so that pattern will make me resent you over time. I am a risk-taker, so I don't mind risking it all and trying new things to make my life advance. You would most likely push a good-paying job on me, instead of supporting my dreams. I don't need that type of energy. Once I conquer the world, I will then bring it home to you and serve you for the rest of my days as your king. Can you dig it?" I say looking directly in her eyes

"That was deep. I love how you put your words together. I just want you to know that every free spirit needs an anchor. When you get tired from taking on the world, I want to be your charger to restore your spiritual battery. I want to be that place of refuge for you. I love that you know where you are going and you know what you want out of life. I want to be led in the right direction by my man. Sorry about the relationship question." she says looking sad.

"You good, in the meantime and between time let's start with a dope friendship. That will be the foundation of our relationship. We still have to get to know one another. I brought you something. It's my favorite book titled *"26 Miles: My Marathon"* written by Jamal Brown. Let me know when you finish it." I say with a stoic expression.

When dealing with a woman who has the potential to be your life partner, you have to be transparent with her. Let her know where she stands. Let her know your visions and dreams. Draw the line in the sand and leave the choice up to her. At the same time educate her with new information to open her mind. Mental orgasms hit differently on a spiritual level. Try it sometime. Thank me later!

She walks me to the door and she says she will see me at school on Monday. I kiss her one more time as I exit the premises.

My phone rings. It's my mother.

"Hey, baby, where are you? Are you okay?"

"It's 7 pm mom, I am on my way home now. See you soon. Love you."

I arrive at home. I hug my mother and make my way to my room. I

immediately doze off. My father comes in and wakes me.
"Son you are sleeping like you got someone pregnant."

"Nah, I am sleeping like I just got some good pussy."

"What did you say?"

"Nothing."

He leaves my room and I fall back asleep only to be awakened by my mother. She has a serious face on. She throws me a box of condoms, Magnum to be exact.

"What are these for?" I ask

"Boy, you are your daddy son! You are a carbon copy. Years ago he used to sleep heavy like you are after I put this goodness on him. I know a spade when I see one! Just be careful out there. Don't bring me any babies."

"Thanks, mom, hit the light on your way out."

Back to sleep, I go.

Chapter 9:
THE TRUTH HURTS

What is understood doesn't have to be explained. If something makes sense to you, never waste time convincing others to jump on board. They will catch up later.

-Brother Brown

It's a quiet Sunday. I'm just chilling in front of my building with Pain. I tell him how my night went with Sue. He is proud of me and glad that I finally got some buns. I laugh it off. Pain's pocket vibrates as he receives an incoming call. It's an invitation to a dice game. We walk around the corner. Many cobras are present and everyone has a handful of cash. The average dice game can last for seven hours.

I really don't like to gamble but Pain gives me money whenever he is winning. I got hot on the dice and ended up winning $300. Pain won $700. I handed Pain a hundred dollar bill and thanked him for throwing me the lifeline. He declined my offer and started to vent to me about missing his father. We are back in front of my building at this point. Pain rarely vents, but when he does, he is sincere.

"I have been feeling kind of off, kid. I miss my pops man. I feel empty growing up fatherless out here. I wonder if he were alive, would anything be different for me? I don't know, probably not. He was the leader of the cobras back in the day I hear, and that's why I am the leader now. I am sort of an heir to his throne in a sense. My mother doesn't really talk about him anymore. When I bring him up she quickly changes the subject. I feel like she is keeping a secret. I think that secret has something to do with the way he died. It just doesn't make sense. How can you be killed in the heart of your own turf and nobody sees anything?"

"She is keeping a secret. All the elders know but we feel that information is too heavy for you to bear, young man." A voice speaks out from behind us.

We twist our necks and look back.

It's Peewee.

He is dressed in all black and wearing a dingy red Chicago Bulls snapback.

"It is about time I tell you the truth. Pain, your father and I used to run together back in the day. We ran the hill! He was the man. I was his enforcer. We were like Two Peas.

"PFFFFFFF!!!!.... RAN THE HILL?"

"Yeah let me explain young bucks. Gather round."

We both laughed at him in unison, then Peewee began to speak.

"I love you Pain, you have been good to me. I must get this information off my chest. It has been plaguing me for some time now. You were the reason your father went so hard. You were his pride and joy. He talked about creating a better life for you often. Then he got pinched. The feds caught him with ten bricks coming back into town. They offered him twenty-five years. He declined the plea and informed the agents about you. He wouldn't miss your childhood for any reason at all. He had to make an executive decision. He decided to give up his 'connect'. The mayor. But the mayor was too connected on all levels. Your father and I found out that the mayor tipped off the feds. Then he put a hit out on your father and had him murdered. Even though your father was high ranking, he was a pawn in the game. The mayor was the mastermind making all the chess moves. When they killed your father, I fell into a depression and started using cocaine. Pain, you are a carbon copy of your father. I see him when I see you. Your mother was the finest thing on the hill back in the day. She was in college when she had you. She wanted to be a nurse at the time. She was taking classes at the college Knowledge's parents teach at. But when your pops died she gave up her dream to take care of you. That's why she is still a CNA at the hospital to this day.

Basically, she put her life on hold to ensure your success, but you are doing the opposite. You are failing her. You are the new pawn in the mayor's game. You are out here risking your freedom for peanuts while he is lining his pockets for retirement. I don't mean to get in your business, but I know he is your 'connect'. And that white boy you hang with. Al, I think his name is. His father was our lawyer back in the day. He was solid as they come. He used to smoke weed heavy, but let me tell you one thing about that cracker; that motherfucker knew how to play the system. He is good in the neighborhood due to his loyalty and history with the Cobras. He saved most of us from receiving long stints in the joint. Enough about him though, let's get back to this crooked ass mayor. I know he is feeding you but you have to get from under his grips. He knows you are dependent on his flow of products in order for the cobras to thrive. He prefers to have it that way. Anyway, I know these cats from Atlantic City moving major weight. I protected them in the joint back in the day. They wouldn't mind expanding their business, matter fact they owe me a favor come to think about it. But in the meantime, you need to devise a plan to take that motherfucker out. His reign is soon to be over, and I can't believe he had your father killed for no reason at all. That was very selfish of him. I know this is a lot for you to take in, but it is all true. With all that being said let me get a fifty of some soft. I'm trying to get high!"

We both just stand there in silence with distorted looks on our faces.

Pain pulls out his black 9mm and cocks it back. He aims at Peewee and says, "Get the fuck out of here with them high rants you be going on."

Peewee doesn't show an ounce of fear. He stands firm with his chest out and continues to speak to Pain.

"You gon' kill the messenger? Honestly, I rather you kill me for telling you, rather than for not conveying this truth. You were going to find out eventually. Well, hurry up and get this shit over with. I'm already dead, Pain! I died when your father died. The quicker you free me from this cell made of flesh, the quicker I can see my boy again. So what is it going to be gangsta? Pull the trigger motherfucker!"

Peewee walks towards Pain staring him indirectly in his eyes with his hands up.

I back up.

Now the barrel is directly between the eyes of Peewee. He closes his eyes and takes a deep breath.

Damn, he's really about to kill Peewee for relaying a message. Pain is a cold motherfucker when he wants to be. Pain looks at me. I shake my head left then right to signal my disagreeing with this action. I could have sworn he was about to shoot Peewee, but instead, he wrapped his arms around him with the pistol still in hand and started to cry.

Peewee starts to cry as he embraces back. I even shed a tear. This was a golden moment. Pain is maturing right before my eyes. As they continue to embrace one another, Pain states some powerful words.

"Thanks for the wake up call, Peewee. This is a losing game I am playing. I have to change in order to change my life. I am going after the mayor. I want his head on a stick. He will pay for what he did. I don't care who gets in my way. His ass is grass! Peewee, I will need you to follow him from a distance and get his schedule down pat. I want to know his every move; I want to catch him when he least expects it. I could get him when I re-up, but I wouldn't make it out that easily. He moves too swiftly."

Pain looks at me.

"Knowledge, now is not the time for a stop the violence speech, or a Malcolm X quote. He killed my father, bro. This has to be done. In the meantime, we need to set up a meeting with the Atlantic City cats. Once I lock them in as my new connection, we will make a move on the mayor."

Peewee stood there for a minute in silence, then looked off in the distance before he came back to the conversation.

"I want you to read something. It's a quote your father used to tell me when we used to beat the blocks up back in the day. I carry it with me wherever I go."

Peewee reaches in his jacket pocket and pulls out a balled-up sticky note. He unravels it and hands it to Pain. It reads:

"For anything illegal, there is a legal side to it"
Get in and get out
Kings don't live long where we from
Check the scoreboard"

Peewee continues to speak.

"Pain, I have lived long enough to see all angles of the game. I have seen the best hustlers have their fifteen minutes of fame then fade out. I'm just lacing you with the history of these cold streets. The streets are undefeated. I lost many friends and family here. Nobody wins in the end. I just hope you know what you are playing for. Develop a plan and work it to manifest your way out. I find solace knowing I have warned you. You are a king. Your strongest muscle is your brain. Think everything through and plan from A to Z. I hope you take heed, young warrior. As for going after the mayor, I will gather up all Intel I can get on him and relay it to you. I am not riding out though. I am too old now. I can't move how I used to. So I will play the fly on the wall with this one."

Pain nods and places the quote in his pocket.

What is understood doesn't have to be explained. If something makes sense to you, never waste time convincing others to jump on board. Actions speak louder than words.

People will get on board later. Put that work in.

I understand that Pain has his mind made up. He is going to kill the mayor with or without my consent. I have to see it from his point of view. If the mayor killed my father to save himself, I would devise a plan to get revenge as well. Going eye for an eye will leave the world blind. Even though that statement is true, I would still even the score. If it were you, what would you do?

CHAPTER 10:
THE MEETING

Age is just a number. You can learn from anyone. Experience comes in all shapes, sizes, and forms. Real should recognize real. Never go off the face card of a good man to vouch for another. Feed everyone with a long spoon. Nobody gets close!

-Brother Brown

After the conversation Pain is still mad about the news that Peewee just laid on him. In an atmosphere full of emotions, there can't be room for logic. I let Pain have his moment. I am the only person who could calm Pain down. Without me, Pain would make many mistakes. Shit, he would probably be dead right now. But that's neither here nor there. As Pain, Peewee, and I stand there outside our building, Pain gives Peewee specific instructions.

"Peewee, I need to meet your 'connect' from Atlantic City as soon as possible. Call him right now and see if he can come to the hill for a business meeting. I can no longer keep making the mayor all this money now knowing where I fall in on his totem pole. I would be a fool to do that. Call him now. Set up a meeting for me."

Peewee nods and makes the call right there on the spot. After the short conversation, Peewee informs Pain that the 'connect' will be in town in about an hour.

The hour goes by quickly. It is now 3 pm in the afternoon. Peewee gets a call and lets Pain know that they are fifteen minutes out. Pain informs Peewee to direct them to come to the courts. We all shoot jump shots while waiting for this individual to arrive. I take the basketball and walk to half-court. Before I could heave the ball towards the rim, the sound of loud engines interrupted my concentration. I turn around and see three white corvettes approaching the courts. I guess Peewee is who he says he is. The sound of car doors shutting is all I hear as I see three Cuban looking men walk up towards the court. Peewee greets the three men with big hugs. I'm guessing they haven't seen Peewee in years based on how they are interacting. Peewee gestures the men towards Pain and I. We all stand there silently.

"Peewee, I didn't drive way down here to play some pickup basketball. You said you wanted to talk business, so let's talk."

He must be the one in charge because he is doing all the talking. He is short with his black hair laid slick to the side. He wore shades and a suit. He had a scar on his forehead. The other men who stood about 6'4 must be his enforcers. They stood with their hands folded.

Peewee begins to speak, as he is simultaneously pointing to Pain.

"Poppy this is Pain. Pain this is Poppy. Pain is the man around here. He runs the hill and he is successful at returning profits in a timely manner. I can personally vouch for him, Poppy. You owe me a favor from back in the day and I am ready to cash in on that. What do you think about putting your product on the streets of the Hill?"

"I don't do business with kids, Peewee, they are bad for business. I do owe you a favor though so this is what I am going to do for you. I will only deal directly with you. You take the product from me and you bring back my money to me. Every time we meet you are to come alone. That is the only way we can do business."

Peewee pleads and vouches for Pain again, but to no avail. Poppy isn't trying to hear it though.

"I know age is just a number. You can learn from anyone, and experience comes in all shapes, sizes, and forms. Real should recognize Real, but I never go off the face card of a good man to vouch for another. I only know you, Peewee, I don't know this kid, and quite frankly I don't want to. I feed everyone with a long spoon. Nobody gets close to me! This logic has kept me in business all my life. I'm sure you understand."

That was some deep shit. Poppy is a businessman and wants no new friends. I like his style and wit. He isn't taking any chances. In the streets, you have to respect the player and the game. That is the only way the solid bridge of loyalty can be built. You can never be caught half stepping that way.

Pain jumps into the conversation.

"I respect your wishes, sir. I can handle 10 pounds of weed per week and 2 kilos. Weekly, I can have your money for you. Thanks for the opportunity. I need that work as soon as possible. Here is $40,000 as a down payment to ensure our business. I don't need a handout; I just need a steady flow. I hope your shit is good as advertised. Peewee will let me know when the shipment arrives. Also, for future references come a little more discreet next time. I like my money relatively quiet, you know. Safe travels back to the city."

Poppy takes the wad of cash and he and his henchmen leave as quickly as they arrived. Pain tells Peewee to tighten up due to his new position. Peewee tells Pain that he will not use cocaine again, and vows to not let Pain down. The bridge has been built.

"Well since I have a new connection, all I have to do is deal with the mayor one more time, and then I am done with him. Peewee, I need you to watch him and learn his schedule so I can devise a plan to avenge my father. Just lay low and play slow. I'll see y'all tomorrow. I am going to meet with the mayor now to give him his money and let him know that I quit. Y'all be easy," says Pain as he walks off.

CHAPTER 11:
THE MESSAGE

I only expect to pass through life but once. If therefore, there be any kindness I can show, or any good thing I can do to any fellow-being, let me do it now, and not defer or neglect it, as I shall not pass this way again.

-William Penn

As we leave the courts I see my father pull up in the parking lot. As Pain and I approach him we notice he had an angry demeanor on his face. He hugs me and goes straight into "Panther mode".

"Pain, I have to lace you. I know what you are doing and I know why. You are playing the hand that you were dealt. But you don't have to. The streets never loved anyone. Everyone dies in the end over senseless reasons that could have been avoided. I know you make a lot of money, and you have power. That is all an illusion. Once they take you out, someone else will be employed to run the hill. You are my son's best friend. I don't want to lose him to some shit you have going on. The game will drain you in the long run. Pimp your money and make it work for you so that you won't be a slave to the block. I just found this information out, so I figured I'd tell you myself."

"You right Mr. T. I can't lie to you. I am the man around here. I hustle to pay my mother's bills and I am saving for college. Knowledge and I are going to Clark Atlanta University when we graduate. The coke I sell is killing the community but the weed is not hurting anyone. Why are you so concerned all of a sudden, Sir?"

"I recently read a book. It was a quote that stuck out to me. It was from this Quaker named William Penn. He stated:

"I only expect to pass through life but once. If therefore, there be any kindness I can show, or any good thing I can do to any fellow-being, let me do it now, and not defer or neglect it, as I shall not pass this way again."

So my reason for relaying this message is that life is short and I can go any day. While I am here it's my duty to warn you of your demise. You aren't the first to run the hill and you won't be the last. Take this message and apply the science. I hope you wake up to your true potential and rise above the project politics. You are like a son to me. I don't want to lose you or my son. When I was a student at Clark Atlanta University, our motto was "Find a way or make one." You will make one; I can see it now, Pain. Play to win. You have been warned. Life is short; I hope you figure it out. I love you like a son."

"Thanks for the free game Mr. T. I'll figure this thing out and make a change. I will see y'all later."

My father and I head home.

Pain heads to see the mayor to re-up for the last time.

Upon arrival, Pain is frisked by the mayor's detail. They take his 9mm. He hands the mayor his weekly profits and waits patiently for his weekly speech.

"Good business is what makes the world turn.", says the Mayor as he counts $60,000 in all one hundred dollar bills. After he counted all the money he pulled out ten pounds of marijuana and two kilos of coke and tells Pain that he will see him next week. Pain pushes the drugs back and tells the mayor that he is done hustling. The mayor had a confused look on his face. Pain dropped some high science on him!

"I am thankful for the opportunity that you have given me. You have helped me stay afloat for years. I mastered the streets and now I want to switch lanes. I want to take my game from the streets to the executive suites. I want to learn the righteous way to make clean money. I am sorry this is so sudden, but I realized the goal of life is to be unreasonably happy. Selling drugs for you won't allow that. In conclusion, I don't even want drugs distributed on the hill anymore. I am cleaning up my neighborhood. I am done selling drugs and poisoning my village."

Pain will never stop hustling. He is just letting the mayor down easy to play it off. The mayor is upset but isn't showing any emotion. No way he is going to let 240k monthly walk away that easily. As Pain heads for the door, the mayor winks at his enforcer. That's code for 'kill in due time'. Pain leaves with two bricks of coke on consignment as a going away gift. Pain doesn't plan on paying for the product since he is plotting to kill the mayor anyway. Pain gets his 9mm back and leaves the premises with the two kilos in his backpack safe and sound. As he heads for the door, the mayor makes a statement that almost ended his life.

"Your father would be proud of the man you have become. We were so close growing up. I miss him."

Pain kept his cool and nodded as he left. He sensed the discernment from the moment he entered the room. History repeats itself, and Pain thinks the mayor wants to give him the same treatment he gave his father. *Game On!*

The game is going to be the game. It is almost impossible to just walk away unscathed. You only make as much as the person teaching you, but once you realize your true worth and potential you must cut off all fat and distractions to ensure success! Easier said than done. It is never easy.

CHAPTER 12: FREQUENCIES FROM THE HOOD

In the underworld, it is easy for a good kid to get trapped in the mad city he resides in. With so many frequencies being thrown at a young man, it is easy to forget what channel you are on. This is why they say everything isn't for everyone. Do the knowledge and weigh the risks. Make it make sense.

-Brother Brown

Sundays are my rest day. I normally just chill and read in my room. Currently, I am in the middle of "The Alchemist" by Paulo Coelho. This is a dope book I can relate to on many levels. Pain calls me and tells me that there is a block party on the hill being thrown by the Cobras. I don't know why they would throw a party in the middle of the winter, but they always throw functions no matter the season. I get dressed and head towards the party. Upon my arrival, I see everybody out at the function. It's crowded. Everyone is out enjoying themselves. I find Pain in the crowd and post up with him in a car owned by one of the cobras. He is with Curtis, the new student. Pain hands me a cup of hot chocolate and tells me to stay warm. He doesn't want me sick for my next game against Buena. Pain has me covered in all angles. A true friend he is indeed.

"Pain I appreciate you for taking me in. I respect your hospitality," says Curtis as he begins to roll a blunt.

"No problem. Just don't cross me, and don't let anyone fuck with Knowledge. Honor those rules and you will be good in my book," says Pain looking him directly in his eyes.

"Too easy," says Curtis as he continues to roll.

As we post up on the vehicle many people start to approach me and show love. The first person to walk up was "Sweets" the neighborhood pimp. He is the wittiest person I have ever met. He likes to have his ego stroked at all times. He is wearing a pink suit with a brown mink coat on. He had on yellow gators with the eyeball on the side. He is clean as they come. Sweets is very "grandiloquent." Yeah, that's the best word to describe his ass.

"Sweets, what's up playa? How are you living Mack daddy, or should I call you the Salmon Assassin with this bright ass suit on?"

"I am blessed, baby. Thanks for asking. Aye Knowledge, you know what I tell the ladies? I pull up and tell them "Yippee I O, let's go", and most women usually jump in my Cadillac, and I tame them. See all women need guidance and I am a human GPS system. See if they knew better, they would do better you feel me? I have the best campaign. They know my name from Maine to Spain, and that's a fact. If you can't dig that, give me my shovel back. You hear me what I say? Sweets is the name and being a pimp is my game!"

Sweets reaches into his coat and hands me two crispy one hundred dollar bills.

"Go get your lady something nice. Take care of her and she will take care of you. Pimp the world son, not just girls."

I thank him as he begins to scold Pain.

"Pop your pistol young player," says Sweets to Pain.

It's a metaphor for "Talk Your Shit" which was a game made up by Pain. Every time they see each other they spit their slickest lines about how they get down. It's pretty funny to see Pain battle the wise men. Sweets came with Eagle, his playa partner whose mouthpiece is sharp as a shark tooth.

Let's check these fools out.

Oh me oh my
Who is that guy?
The Ladies Man
They call me Eagle
I'm the flyest in the sky
Also the hood historian
I have seen it all
From the rise to the fall
Still I Run
Because I am smooth
I take a bitch and elevate her
You can't compete
Where you can't reach
I'm in the sky
The name is Eagle
Nice to meet you

Eagle came hard. Let's hear Sweets pop his pistol.

I tell a bitch
It's a damn shame
If she don't know my name
They call me Sweets
My hand stretches far
I am everywhere like air
On a bitch ass, like grass
If she doesn't have my cash
I'm in this game to win
I have to watch out for snakes
And being backstabbed by friends
In the end we all die
So every day I thank God I am alive
I have a collection of nice things
Pimping has been good to me
I wouldn't have it any other way.
The name is Sweets
Nice to meet you

Sweets never disappoints when he is spitting. Last but not least, let's hear Pain pop his pistol.

Pain is the name
That is all I bring
Tsss Tsss Tsss
Cobra Gang
Observation is the source of my knowledge
The Hill is my kingdom
I will reign forever
Until I go to college
Yeah, me and Knowledge
Like the alligator
I will see you later
When I return
I am running for mayor
It was written
I strive for peace
But never forget
Pain is the name
That is all I bring
Nice to meet you

"You are getting better young Pain. Keep it up. Now watch the back of my head get small," says Sweets as he and Eagle step off.

"I am going to start a #PopYourPistolChallenge on the gram. I am sure it will go viral." Pain mumbles to himself.

Who do you think won? I think Eagle did. He killed them with that one *"you can't compete where you can't reach"* line.

Anyways. A pimp is an acronym. Pimp stands for "person interested in making profits" according to Sweets. In that case, shit we all are pimps. Who doesn't want to make money? In the distance, I hear someone yell "Yo cuz, Yo Knowledge". I look around until I get to the source of the voice. It's Jersey walking with Bone. Jersey is walking with a cane. He is still recovering from being shot in the leg. He walks up and I hug him and tell him I am glad he is okay. He tells me he has turned over a new leaf.

"You still hustling, cuz? What do you have on the market these days?" I asked while sipping on my hot chocolate.

"Fuck hustling and fuck them streets! I just put in an application with the City of Bridgeton. The few bucks I was chasing in the streets weren't worth my life. I am going to get a job and stay out of the way. That was my wake-up call. I could have easily killed the people that shot me but I remember what you told me. A wise man once asked,

"Why do life for taking a life that wasn't worth nothing anyway?"

In the streets, most people straighten up after they get shot or robbed. Others take on a sense of invisibility and feel untouchable since they feel they cheated their death date. I am glad Jersey took my advice and applied it.

White Boy Al joins us as we continue to post on the vehicle. He rolled a blunt and he and Pain began to smoke. Pain noticed Detective Clark in plain clothes and quickly put out the blunt and threw it.

Detective Clark walks up with his chest out in his macho stance. He is the same detective that has been trying to take the cobras down any chance he gets. He is what you consider an Uncle Tom. He has traded on his fellow man since he received his badge.

His supervisor, Captain Jackson, accompanies him. She comes out to the field during big events only. She is thick as hell and has a distinct mole on her lip. Sweets have been trying to put her under his management for years but to no avail. She is as tough as they come. She is from the Hill so she knows the game. She just happens to be on the other side of the fence. She went to school with my father back in the day. I hear she was a softball legend.

Anyways Pain is too smart for them and their *by-the-book* methods.

"Pain, I smell a strong odor coming from this area. Give me the weed and I will not arrest you. Hurry up, I don't feel like doing paperwork." Detective Clark says as he places his hands on his weapon.

"I think a skunk was killed around here earlier, that has to be the only reason why that aroma is present at this particular location."

Detective Clark gets mad and frisks Pain. He finds no drugs, but a bunch of cash. He asked for the source of the cash and Pain said that Detective Clark's mother gave it to him.

"I am basically retired, your mother gives me her monthly pension. I am her cub and she is my cougar. She is under good management though. You don't have to worry." Pain says as he shakes my hand and laughs.

Nas said it best on his song titled "Represent" when he stated, *"My work is on the streets so the jakes will never stop it!"*

As long as the pushers have product Pain will forever profit. That is the best way to stay ahead of the curve. He can never get caught red-handed with the product.

Detective Clark walks off angrily. Captain Jackson told me good luck at my next game. Man if I hit that I will be the man. No man in the land has claimed them buns. Dreams do come true you know.

Pain notices the neighborhood pastor exiting the corner store on the block. He motions him over. The pastor approaches.

"Ayo Knowledge, watch this. This is how you expose a fraud. Take notes"

We greet the pastor with pounds, and Pain begins to ask for a favor from the pastor.

"Oh beloved, Reverend Davis, my mother needs a return on her investment. We are short on the rent this month. She has been coming to your church for the past five years, and she pays fifty bucks via offering on a weekly basis, in return for a mysterious blessing from the good lord. Over the past five years, she has contributed exactly $12,000 to the church only to be left currently scrambling for bill money. So can you help us or not? The rent is only $700."

"Tell your mother to call me, and I will pray a powerful financial prayer with her. The Lord will bless her with an abundance of cash." stutters Reverend Davis as he looks for any reason to escape the conversation.

Pain asked one more question. With his hands still folded he continues his interrogation.

"Why when your church needs help, you ask the congregation for money, but when the congregation needs help you quickly resort to prayer as the only solution?

Reverend Davis receives a phone call and rushes off.

"God bless you, young men." He says as he walks away. Perfect timing I guess.

When you ask questions that go entirely against what the benefiter is benefiting from, you will make him angry. He will try to cease the conversation very quickly. Most pastors sell hope, Hope is more profitable than drugs, and it comes with less of a headache. Since time is the new money, no wonder why they only work one day a week. The profits they see on that one day will fund their second lives all week. Pastors will ride the hope wave hoping to never hit the shore. Will they swim forever?

"God loves us all."

Reverend Davis has been running that same line longer than the cable guy! Fuck him and that religion. He can save that game for what's his name!

After I calm down, a group of girls walks by. Pain being Pain, yells out:

"Ayo, look at the turd cutter on, shorty! I bet when she fart it goes BOOOOOOOM!"

White Boy Al and I laugh and dap each other up. Pain's face gets serious as he hones in on the female.

"I knew I recognized that face. That's Cinnamon, the adult film star," says Pain.

Pain walks toward her screaming her name to get her attention. She stops and they begin to converse.

"Pain, right?" she asks.

"Yeah, that's what they call me. How do you know my name?" Pain asks nervously.

"I left the Hill when you were a baby. After your father was murdered, I moved to Los Angeles and have been there ever since. I used to traffic products for the cobras. Your father was a good man, and he took care of his people. I hear you are running things now, I have been hearing good things about you. Keep it up," responds Cinnamon.

"Damn, you have been around for a while. Well, I am the man around here, but I don't praise titles. Oh yeah, I ran over to thank you for your service," says Pain.

"Thank me for my service? Please elaborate. I am confused because I am neither a firefighter nor police officer. Those are the people who need to be thanked," replies Cinnamon.

"They get thanked all the time, but I want to thank you for getting me through some lonely nights before I started getting some. We are always quick to thank first responders but scared to show love to the porn stars who fulfill our wildest fantasies and desires. I'm a huge fan. Keep up the good work. Maybe when I get older, I can come visit California with my best friend Knowledge," says Pain with confidence in his voice.

"Anytime you want to visit, just give me a heads up. Cobras are everywhere like air. When you get older you will see the organization for what it really is. But thanks for showing me love and supporting me. Here is my number, call me when you want to visit. Tsss, Cobra for life," says Cinnamon as she walks off.

Pain heads back towards us posting up. He had a huge smile on his face.

"Knowledge, we are good in California now. I just got us free room and board out there," says Pain.

"My man Pain, smooth as glass when pursuing the ass," I say sarcastically.

"This is business right here brother. It's not even like that," says Pain.

Before I could respond. A strong odor of marijuana blew by. We looked around to find the source of the scent. We found it. It was coming from Smoking Reggie who was approaching us. We call him "Smoking Reggie" because he is always smoking. Plus, whenever we see him he drops some deep philosophy.

"What's up, Reggie, I have a question for you."
"Speak on it, Knowledge"

"Why are you always smoking? Are you ever sober? What is marijuana to you? I swear you are higher than the greeting."

"Ah. You thought you caught me slipping, huh? I am always ready to defend my dear marijuana. Weed is the answer to peace on earth. If it weren't for the weed, the people would be in a major frenzy. Honestly, I think they would purge daily. You see weed is only illegal because it makes a ton of money for the so-called people in power. If they legalize it, then the government would only make money from the taxes made on it. I don't think the government will ever take a pay cut son. I don't care if it is legal or not, I am going to smoke regardless. I just want to get high and live my life on my own terms. The world better be happy I smoke because if I didn't I would probably be in someone's bushes. So in conclusion, weed is the answer to peace on earth! My name is Reggie and that is my Ted Talk."

Pain and Al dap Reggie up and tell him that he needs a Nobel Peace Prize for that perfect breakdown. In the hood, there is always a group of rebels who could care less about the system. They fit in nowhere and are comfortable being outsiders. I respect Reggie because he knows who he is and doesn't try to be anything or anyone else.

Before Reggie walked off, he told us something astounding.

"I must be transparent with you all. I use drugs for recreational purposes. I want to tell you to never use drugs when desperate. If so, you will accelerate your self-destruction."

I don't smoke, and I don't think I ever will. I get high by dunking on people and playing basketball.

The street we are occupying is blocked off. I notice everyone clearing the road and making way for an all-black Range Rover to enter.

"Who the fuck is that?" We all ask in unison.

The vehicle enters the street and pulls up directly in front of us. The back window slowly lowers and to my surprise, it is Brother Brown the Author! He instructs me to jump in. He gives Pain a head nod, and Pain takes his hand off of his nine. I jumped in the truck and began to thaw out. It was cold outside on the block. He had the heat blasting.

"What's up, Brother Brown? Are you here promoting your next book or something?"

"No, I am here to support the cobras and this block party. I used to be a cobra back in the day, but I snapped out that gang-banging mentality when I moved away. The logic of a gangbanger is irrational to the ways of the working world. I had to learn the hard way. When I first started writing books I was famous in this town but I wasn't loved. Paulo Coelho states 'No man is a prophet in his own land. His hometown will only accept him once the world does.' So with that being said never waste your time entertaining small minds."

"That's some real shit. I am actually reading one of his books right now. So why did you leave the Hill?"

"Yeah his books are cool, but start reading some of Hill Harper's books. Start with *Letters to a Young Brother,* which is a good one for young brothers like yourself. But to answer your question, I left because I became too big for the Hill. My dreams and ambitions went over the heads of everyone I encountered. I remember when I wrote 26 Miles, I had readers lined up around the block. The police raided my apartment after I did a local book signing. They thought I was selling dope. I was! It was intellectual dope via my books, the dope that heals and not kills. I was wholesaling my books to street dealers and they would make triple in profits. Everyone was eating. My profit was the positive feedback the people gave me for writing. After the raid, I sued the police for $100,000 and used all that money to move away. I support the town from afar. I have been hearing good things about you. I hear you have an opportunity to attend Clark Atlanta for school. I hope you plan to attend. I will cover all costs for your tuition if you do. I still have a few connections there still. You are the neighborhood hero. I am here to give you reassurance to stay on the path of righteousness. This world is yours, kid, go get that motherfucker and put your name on it."

"I appreciate this game you are giving me. I will definitely take heed. Can you spit a poem for me? I love your poetry!"

He spit one right off the back.

*I AM A COBRA FOR LIFE
YOU ASK ME WHY I LEFT THE BLOCK
IT WAS BECAUSE
THAT SHIT WAS GETTING HOT*

*I SEEN A MAN START A CLOTHING LINE
HE ASKED HIS FOLKS TO BUY IT
THEY TOLD HIM TO WAIT ON IT
MONTHS LATER WHEN HE DIED
THEY BOUGHT T-SHIRTS WITH HIS FACE ON IT*

*HONESTLY
THAT WASN'T GENUINE
BECAUSE WHEN YOU WANT TO SUPPORT SOMEONE
YOU SHOULD DO IT WHILE THEY ARE LIVING
I USED TO PLAY THE BLOCK LIKE I WOULDN'T LIVE AGAIN*

*I'VE SEEN FRIENDS CATCH BIDS, AND ADAPT TO THAT
PRISON SHIT
THEIR KIDS GOT ACCUSTOMED TO THAT VISIT SHIT
I PRAY I DON'T HAVE TO EVER DO THAT TO MY KIDS MY
MAN*

*I REALIZED WE CAUGHT UP IN A CYCLE,
IT'S A VICIOUS ONE
WE AREN'T TAUGHT TO GET A TITLE
ONLY TO GET A GUN*

"In conclusion, Knowledge, remember that you don't have to sell drugs or commit crimes to have nice things. Look at me as an example. I have bought a house and this car cash! I used all the profits from my books to fund it. My money is clean. The white man hates it but he has to respect it. I don't need him for me to prosper. The goal is to be debt-free and unreasonably happy. I have to go, keep up the good work. I will be in touch. Stay away from 'the project politics. Tell your man's, Pain, to hop in," instructs Brother Brown.

It caught me off guard. I didn't think he knew who Pain was. I do as instructed.

"Yo Pain, get in the car bro," I say to him as I step out.

"Why?" he asks as he enters the vehicle.

I am speechless as I exit the car. I took his business card and stuffed it in my jacket. As I sat back on the block I started to realize that the world was bigger than The Hill and that the world should know about *KNOWLEDGE!* I needed to see someone win that was from here. If he can do it so can I. Sweets always tells me to take my game from the streets to the executive suites. I get what he was saying now.

"What's going on, Sir?" asks Pain as he looks around in the backseat.

"Pain, right?" asks Brother Brown while rubbing his chin.

"Allow me to introduce myself. My name is Brother Brown. I used to be the most dangerous man to walk The Hill. I was with all that came with the game at one point. Until one day I decided I wanted more out of life. I made a move for the better, and it worked out for me. I was one of your father's wolves. I was third in line, right under Peewee. Yeah, we ran the Hill. I have been hearing good things about you. I am here to tell you to work on your life's plan, Life after The Hill. Your father used to tell me all the time this one particular quote.

> *"For anything illegal, there is a legal side to it*
> *Get in and get out*
> *Kings don't live long where we're from*
> *Check the scoreboard"*

Develop a way out as soon as possible. Here is my number. Call me sometime. Now join me in stating The Cobra Creed," says Brother Brown.

> *I pledge allegiance to the Cobras*
> *The mission is always first*
> *I won't stop until it's over*
>
> *I am my brother's keeper*
> *If I have a problem with him*
> *I will address it*
> *I will not let pride divide us*
>
> *Dear Lord,*
> *If I make a mistake*
> *And fall short of your glory*
> *Forgive me*
> *You were once lost*

So you say
But
If it's my time to go
&
I don't survive the night
I just want to say
"Thanks"
For letting me live and die
As a cobra!
Tsssssss...

COBRA FOR MOTHERFUCKING LIFE!

Pain exited the car laughing. I asked him what Brother Brown wanted with him.

"Nothing, he was just introducing himself," says Pain as he returns to post up.

Brother Brown tells his driver to park the car and steps out his vehicle. He finds Peewee in the mix and they begin to converse.

"Do my eyes deceive me? Am I dreaming? Is that my Brown Brother? Hold up let me pinch myself so make sure I'm not dreaming. What's up man!" says Peewee, very excited.

They embrace.

"Wake up baby, It's me in the flesh! Blink, you aren't dreaming. You know my motto. There are many brown brothers but there is only one Brother Brown. How are you doing Peewee? You are looking good. You look clean," says Brother Brown smiling.

"Yeah man. I put that stuff down. Pain put me in position so I have to be on point 24/7," says Peewee.

"I just met this Pain you speak of. He seems pretty sharp. Keep him out of trouble. How's Knowledge doing?" says Brother Brown. "He is just like his pops. I will keep him close and out the way. Knowledge is good. He has the best pull-up jumper I have seen since you played in the doghouse. He has a good chance to go to the league. Duke wants him but he has his mind set on Clark Atlanta University," says Peewee.

"As he should. If they want the best, they will have to come watch us at our HBCUs. That is another conversation for another day. Let me go, I have to make a few moves. It was good seeing you brother. I'll keep you in my prayers. Tss, Cobra for Life," says Brother Brown as he walks back to his vehicle.

"Tss. Cobra For Life," says Peewee as he heads over to Pain and I.

See in the underworld, it is easy for a good kid like myself to get trapped in the mad city he resides in. With so many frequencies being thrown at me, it is easy to forget what channel I am on. This is why they say everything isn't for everyone. Do the knowledge and weigh the risks against the rewards. Make it make sense. I am no pimp like Sweets, I am no gang member like Pain, I am no hustler like Jersey, and I am no scamming preacher like Rev Davis. I am what I am. An educated athlete named Knowledge who will make it on my own terms. Nothing more nothing less! I am glad there is no school tomorrow. I can rest and mentally prepare for the big game against Buena.

I dap all the cobras up and make my way home. As I approach my building I see a man lying out on the ground with a bottle of whiskey in his palm. He is wearing a black hat and an army coat. I wasn't going to speak but he started the conversation.

"Young man, I don't know you but I have to warn you. A black man has no place in the white man's army. You stay in school as long as you can. Stay away from the military. I have seen the ugly face of war. I can't sleep at night. I have PTSD. The VA keeps denying my claims. So until I get my money, I am broke. America has used me, and then abused me. In the civilian world, most of these companies are offering to buy your time, kid, the real question is how much are you willing to sell yours for? Let's say you had five hours to live, and someone came along and offered you a million dollars an hour for three hours of work. Would you take it? Hell to the naw. In conclusion, all I am saying is that it is never enough money to replace time. Live your life young man because we are only here for a stint. Life is shorter than the legs on a cricket. Oh, by the way, my name is Barry. I will see you around, kid. TSSSS, Cobra For Life."

I wish Pain were here for this lecture. Barry said some real shit. I store the information in my mental Rolodex and head to my room. I'm beat. I need to recharge.

CHAPTER 13:
LIMBO

Never turn your back on your people for an occupation, because when that occupation turns its back on you, you can no longer return home. You will forever be labeled a trader and will be forced to live the rest of your days as an outsider in limbo.

-Brother Brown

The block party ended in peace. There were no fights and no one was shot. That's great to hear with all the bullshit going on these days. The Hill is silent as everyone is home preparing to tackle the next day.

Meanwhile, Detective Clark heads into the precinct as the end of his shift approaches. Upon him entering his office he is called into the Mayor's office. Once inside he felt a weird tension in the atmosphere as he sat there silently. He knows he is about to be scolded about his lack of results when it comes to taking down the Cobras. Over the span of two years, he hasn't made any big arrests and only has gotten the department sued for harassment. Pain used to tell him that he was a pawn in the police department's game, but Detective Clark is numb to giving advice. He has a big ego and a very arrogant posture. The badge powers his entire existence. The badge covers up most of his insecurities. That's neither here nor there. Let me get back to the story.

As Detective Clark sat there, the Major began to speak.

"Detective Clark, we are removing you from Operation Cobra. We have a new detective heading the investigation. You know Detective Saunders I believe."

Detective Clark is taken aback by the statement.

"This is some bullshit, sir! I am the best man for the "OPERATION COBRA" assignment. No offense, but he can't handle the Cobras. They are very close-knit. It is damn near impossible to infiltrate them. Nobody wants to give up information. The members would rather do life and die before they give each other up. They are as loyal as they come. You would think they were under an occult or something. I couldn't bribe them with money or freedom. None of my tactics worked yet. To be honest, Detective Saunders will stick out like a sore thumb out there. Nobody will take him seriously due to his skin color. These cobras are smart. Pain is not to be taken lightly."

"Thanks for the Intel Clark, but we will take it from here. I will give you a briefing on your new assignment tomorrow morning", says the Major.

"I have risked my life day in and day out for this fucking police department. I feel used and abused. I am starting to feel as though I was used as a tool to lock up my own kind, and now that the investigation is drying up, you are washing your hands with me. That's not fair, but that is how the cookie crumbles I guess. Duly noted," replies Detective Clark still upset.

"Whelp, have a good night Clark. I have to bring Saunders up to speed with the investigation. Bring me your field notes," says the Major.

Detective Clark walked away livid. Mumbling to himself he pulls his phone out as he exits the precinct. Once in the car he scrolled through his contact list and called his cousin Dave. Dave was an older cat who had a successful construction business in Bridgeton. Detective Clark asked Dave if he had any open positions. Dave replied,

"You are the police, cuz, you don't want to do this backbreaker work. But to answer your question I have a foreman position open that I am looking to fill immediately. Starting pay rate is $22 an hour, so if you are serious about quitting the force let me know. I have to go. Call me tomorrow. cuz."

Detective Clark hangs up and drives to The Hill in his personal car. He spots Pain and some cobras loitering in front of the corner store. Pain and the cobras are trying to see who is in the car because they don't recognize it. Detective Clark hopped out and approached them cool and calm.

"What are you doing Pain? Are you young men out here hustling?" asks Detective Clark yawning.

"Na, I'm just standing here congregating with the fellas. About these drugs, you think I sell. You have been after me for the past two years and haven't turned up any results. I told you I am not a drug dealer," says Pain with a stoic expression.

"Cut the shit Pain! You and I both know who you are and what you do. By the way, I have been reassigned to another case. The department feels as though I have been wasting money and resources because I haven't yielded any results or arrests during the investigation. I have to give it to you; you are pretty smooth. I tip my hat to you," says Detective Clark.

"I do not take compliments from men, but you can tell Captain Jackson I said hello with her fat ass!" says Pain as he daps up a few of his crewmembers.

"Let me be frank with you son. There is a new detective named Saunders. He is now investigating the Cobras for distributing narcotics. He is a white guy who has it out for people like you," says Detective Clark.

One of the cobras remembers the name and tells Pain that he was pulled over by him yesterday and vouches for the character description given by Detective Clark. Pain asked why he was the recipient of all this good information. He thought it came with a catch.

"There is no catch. I was simply used to locking up young men that look like me. When the arrest rate dropped, I suddenly turned into the bad guy in the eyes of my superiors. I am about to quit soon. Also, I want to inform you that my cousin has a construction company that pays pretty well. If any of the cobras would like a job, let me know. I will put in a word on your behalf," says Detective Clark

See Detective Clark turned his back on his people in the name of the badge. His badge made him blind to the trauma and struggles that people of color deal with day in and day out. Once he woke up to what was really going on in the grand scheme of things, he had to make a decision. To win back the hearts and minds of the community he decided to come with vital information that would benefit their pockets. Information from the inside is vital for any operation to thrive.

Pain wasn't trying to hear it though. He wasn't convinced that Detective Clark was being sincere. Looking him dead in the eyes, Pain asked.

"How do I know that you aren't trying to set me up? How can I confirm that you are sincere and this information is valid?"

"They know about the stash spot on Giles St. When we were about to raid the house, we got a call about a shooting simultaneously. So the only reason we didn't raid was because he had to expend all our troops. You got lucky. I'm sure that's the reason you closed shop the very next day. What's done is done though. Nowadays, I could care less what you do. Just be careful. If I hear of anything you will be the first to know. After I put in my 2 weeks tomorrow, the clock starts. Until I turn in this badge and gun I am your inside man." says Detective Clark.

The statement was one hundred percent facts. Pain told me he had to switch the logistics up a few days ago. He felt something in the air. Pain couldn't deny the truth.

"Who would have thought it was an actual *brother* in there the whole time behind that vest. I knew he was in there somewhere. Good looking out on the Intel. I will see you around. Watch your back and keep your eyes open. Believe it or not, there is a target on your back now," says Pain in a smooth voice.

After the conversation, both parties went their separate ways. As Pain headed to his house he told his cobras he wants them to remember a particular quote.

"I know y'all are wondering why I even entertained him. Time has a way to reveal to us who we are. As the world turns, we live and we learn. As long we live, we will always have a chance to right our wrongs. As for Detective Clark, he will do whatever it takes to get his face card back up to par in the community; and at any cost. Remember that gentlemen."

The Cobra all nodded their heads and said, "that's real shit" in unison. Pain reached in his pocket and called me to see if I was good.

"Ayo, Knowledge where you at kid?" he asked, sounding concerned.

"I'm home bro, just chilling. What's up? Is everything good?" I ask

"Yeah, I am Meghan Good! I didn't want shit though. Just making sure you were safe bro and to let you know that I love you. Get some rest kid. I will call you in the morning. Tsss, Cobra for life." says Pain in a genuine voice.

"Love you too you bucket head motherfucker. Gone somewhere with that sentimental shit. Hit me in the morning though. Over and out." I say as I roll over in my bed and pass out.

CHAPTER 14:
RULES TO RULE

Haters are a part of the game. It doesn't matter what game you play or what lane you are in. When things are going good, everyone is happy, but when you begin to walk on the path to individualism, the game gets tricky. Stagnated people never want to see people close to them prosper. My advice is to feed people with a long spoon so they can't see the ingredients in your kitchen. A king must always know the rules to rule.

-Brother Brown

It's Monday. School was canceled due to a teacher's conference. I figure I take this day and chill out. As I lie across my bed and rub my feet together I ponder about Sue. What is she up to? I pause my video game and call her up. She answered the first ring! I got straight to the point.

"What's up love, I hope you are free later, I want to come over and redeem myself," I say while lying on my back with my feet in the air.

A good conversation will have your body deformed and tangled, you know. I thought I was smooth until she checked me.

"Look at you, Knowledge. You got a teaspoon of sex and lost your damn mind. I knew this would happen. Well, you aren't getting any more of me until Bridgeton wins the state championship this year. So take all that sexual energy you have and redirect that shit into your game. I'll come to the Hill and get your rebounds while you shoot free throws if you would like."

Damn. She just played me. I thought I was smooth with it. I guess not. To be honest, Sue is everything I need. She demands respect and will not settle. She keeps me on my toes. Her personality is dope as well. I hit the jackpot if you ask me. Anyway, I grant her wishes and tell her to meet me at the court in an hour. As soon as I hang up, a text message from Pain comes through to my phone. It read,

"Look out your window."

I do just that. I ruffled through my curtains and proceeded to lookout. I see Pain bouncing a basketball. I lift the window and immediately Pain starts talking shit.

"Fuck that video game you playing, come to the court so I can dust you off kid."

I turn off the game, put on my shoes, and head downstairs. When I arrive Pain attempts to shake my hand. I fake the handshake and reach for the ball and steal it away. We laugh it off and head to the court. We have a court right in the center of cobra territory. We can play here and not have to worry about looking over our shoulders. You would be a fool to try something here.

"Make ten shots bro! Keep shooting until you make ten." Pain says as he stands under the rim.

Swish after swish, I make ten three-pointers in a row. On the last one, I posed for the imaginary cameras. After I come off my high, I see Pain approaching me quickly in an aggressive manner.

"Play me one on one superstar," he says as he hands me the ball and drops into his defensive stance.

He can't be serious. Pain is probably high; his jitteriness is giving him away. I ask if he is okay. He nods his head up and down to confirm. I know what he is doing. He is trying to sharpen my mental toughness. I have a big game coming up against Buena next week. They are undefeated and reigning champions. They have a crazy student section that always harasses the opposing team's best players.

Let me get back to the one-on-one with Pain. I let him have the ball first. Pain has one move he knows. His pull-up jumper is his only asset. He attempts to shoot and I block the ball towards the fence. I saved it before it went out of bounds. We checked up and I made three threes in a row. They were all net!

"THAT'S SIX NOTHING! You can't see me, kid?" I say as we check for game point.

I get the ball and stare off into the distance. Pain is nosey and turns around to inquire. When he turns back around I am halfway to the basket. I toss the ball off the backboard and dunk it as hard as I can. Pain fell for the oldest trick in the book.

"GAME!" I yell as I hang on the rim.

"Hell yeah, that's what I am talking about. Buena isn't going to know what hit them on Wednesday!" Pain says as we shake hands.

"Let's go get some Gatorade from the store. We have to hurry back because Sue is coming up here to hang out soon."

Pain joins me.

As we stroll to the store I thank Pain for his friendship and loyalty. It's rare that people stay down these days. Pain tells me I don't have to thank him. As we get closer to the store Pain gets a call on his burner phone and tells me to go ahead into the store. He probably has a sale to make. As I walk off I hear him on the phone in the distance.

"I got you, bro, give me fifteen minutes. I am handling something at the moment. I will hit you when I am finished."

Sweets was standing in front of the store. A young lady dressed in a skirt walked up as we conversed. At first, I thought it was one of his ladies, but I found out it was an old friend. I overheard his conversation. Sweets was talking his normal good old "Sweet nothings" to her. Man, he is sharp with the word play.

"I haven't seen you lately, Sweets. Where have you been daddy?" says the female.

"If you see me every day, something is wrong baby. I have been looking for you too though love. I have to tell you something," replies Sweets in a smooth tone.

"Cut it out. I'm here now, so what's up?" she replies with curiosity in her eyes.

"I know you've been wondering where I've been. I've been searching myself to find love within. I came back to reality to let you know that I got a thing for you, and I can't let go. My friends wonder what is wrong with me. I tell them that I'm in a daze from your love, you see? I'm serious. I came back to let you know that I have a thing for you and I can't let go. I have a vision for us. Choose me as your captain, and I'll steer you to the Promised Land."

Damn, I don't know how he comes up with this shit but it always works. The young female reached into her crotch area and pulled out a wad of cash and handed it to Sweets and walked off.

"Damn Sweets, where do you get these lines from?" I ask laughing hard.

"Between me and you, I borrowed that from a song by Bobby Caldwell. These young women don't know anything about good music. They are lost in the sauce, and I am the chef. She thought I was serious. She is under my management now. Here is $200 to keep you bouncing that ball young man. Make sure you stay safe," says Sweets as he walks off towards Pain.

I open the battered door of the corner store and head for the cooler. I grab two Gatorades and some barbecue chips. As I approach the register, I greet Mr. Bo. He has owned this corner store my entire existence.

"What's up, Mr. Bo?
"I'm fine, thanks for asking."

Pain walks in. Mr. Bo makes a joke and calls us twins due to us having black hoodies on. Pain pulls out a wad of cash and thumbs through twenty-dollar bills in search of some singles. Sue calls and I head outside for some privacy.

"Hey Knowledge, I am close to you. I am about 15 minutes away. I am getting dropped off in an Uber."

I tell her I will stay on the phone with her to make sure she isn't riding with a creep. She thanked me. She asked if I missed her. Before I could answer, an all-black Escalade pulled up very quickly. The window rolled down slowly, and a voice yelled out "FUCK YOU PAIN, YOU ARE A DEAD MAN."

Pain exits the store with the bag of items. He notices the escalade and drops the bag.

"RUN KNOWLEDGE!"

I ran off fast as I could towards my building, which was up the street. I feel bullets whizzing by my head. I hear glass shattering as car alarms go off. I hear people screaming and running to find cover. I jumped behind a trashcan and looked back towards the store. I see Pain running towards me with his gun in hand. Once he reaches me, he shoots towards the escalade. The escalade skirted off.

"C'mon bro, we got to go kid", that was one of the people from the mayor's detail. I recognized him from when I used to re-up. I think the mayor put a hit out on me since I don't hustle for him anymore."

As I attempt to walk, I quickly feel a sharp pain in my stomach. I look down and my hoodie. It is soaked with blood.

"Pain, I think I'm hit!"

Pain lifts my shirt and we both look to see if I was hit. We notice two bullet holes in my abdomen. They are gushing with blood. I feel my throat closing, and blood is spilling from my mouth.

"I am getting cold, Pain."

"HELP! HEEEELP!" Pain screams as he looks around for help.

I blink slowly as I dose in and out of consciousness. I notice two cobras running up from the turf.

Pain tells one of them to take his weapon and to get out of the area. He tells the other one to call the police. He shakes me to keep me awake but I am drifting towards the light. Pain cries as he holds me tight in his arms. Police sirens are heard in the distance.

"C'mon Knowledge! Stay with me, King. Don't leave me out here!"

It's too late. I took my last breath in Pain's arms. I slowly pass away with my eyes wide open aimed at the sky. Pain closes them as he kisses me on my forehead.

"NOOOOOOOOOOOO!"

The cobra that called the police is standing speechless. By this time the news traveled fast, and everyone is crying at the crime scene. Pain is still holding me. In the midst of sirens, he hears a low voice. Confused, he starts to look for where it was coming from.
"Hello, hello, Knowledge," a muffled voice says

Pain looks down and notices that it was Sue. My phone never hung up. Pain picked up my phone with his hand trembling.

"Sis, Knowledge is gone! I am so sorry Sue."

The police arrive and attempt all the tricks of the trade to revive me. Nothing worked. I am pronounced dead at the scene. Damn, I died for nothing. In my opinion, that is the worst way to die, for nothing! I had so much potential and was destined to rise above this madness. I died for no cause, I died defending no mission, and my death was a simple result of project politics.

All of this could have been avoided with an isolated conversation. Pimping Ken said it best; Conversation runs the nation. He never lied.

See the mayor put money on Pain's head because Pain wised up and freed himself from his hamster wheel. Pain had all the logical reasons to cut ties with the mayor due to the news from Peewee. This was personal; I don't think it was business. They were gunning for each other for reasons they both deemed logical. When two parties vow to take out each other by any means, innocent people always get hurt. Look at me for example.

The mayor was a hater but haters are a part of the game. It doesn't matter what game you play or what lane you are in. When things are going good, everyone is happy, but when you begin to walk on the path to individualism, the game gets tricky. Stagnated people never want to see people close to them prosper forward. My advice is to feed everyone with a long spoon so they can't see the ingredients in your kitchen. A king must always know the rules to rule.

CHAPTER 15:
NO GLUE, NO CLUE

In every hood, there is always one person who is destined to rise above the madness and make it out. But when things go awry like the plans of mice and men, the hood suffers. When the community loses its glue, the citizens have no clue what to do!

-Brother Brown

The Hill has been silent since my absence. Many questions are flooding the atmosphere about my death. None of the citizens of Bridgeton can believe of all people, I have passed away.

Neither can you. It happens to the best of us, believe it or not. I was senselessly killed due to factors beyond my control before I could reach my true potential. The neighborhood has a black cloud over it since I no longer walk the streets. I was the glue that held everything together, and I was the light that kept hope alive for the hopeless. Without my positive spirit, the town has relapsed into their old ways and actions.

My parents took off work for a while. They couldn't take losing their only son. They have been in the house since they received the call. My mother sits in my room and cries herself to sleep from time to time. My father has to stay strong and hold back his tears. He has to suffer in silence and be strong for the community.

Jersey heard about the news while at work. He quit on the spot and quickly found Pain. He tells him to keep him abreast when he retaliates, and that he is riding for me. Pain nods his head, but he is falling apart slowly. He is struggling to run the Cobras. He is short on his re-up with Poppy. He apologizes for the count being off.

Poppy tells Pain, "Lay off the streets for a while, get your head together, and then business will resume. I like you kid, I just can't take any more losses. Let me know when this blows over! Be safe!"

In times of turmoil, I was the one Pain would turn to. He has no one now. I hope he applies the science of the lessons I taught him while I was living.

Peewee relapses. He couldn't get any coke from the cobras and ended up shopping outside the territory on the North side. I am sure Pain will be upset due to this act. Pain needed Peewee for information on the mayor. Since my tragic death, all that shit went out the window. "Vices" and "faith in change" are the two forces that hold down an addict. He must pick a road and stay the course if he wants to succeed.

Wiz took my death the worst in my opinion. The next day he closed his barbershop and moved back to Texas to where he originated. He could no longer reside in a city that killed its own neighborhood hero.

White Boy Al is no stranger to violence. He has seen his share of death growing up here. He is numbed by my death and just stays home and smokes himself to sleep so he can escape reality.

My team had back-to-back games the upcoming week. They lost to Buena by 23 points and then to Wildwood by 22. The state championship goal is tarnished. My teammates gave it their all but to no avail. They needed me out there, but I was in a casket for no damn reason at all.

Pain told my father what exactly happened the day I was shot. My father was very upset about the news. All that 'love your fellow brother' logic went out the window.

"Handle It! Do what you have to do. I want him killed and his head on a stick. Let me know when the deed is done. Be safe, Pain."

In every hood, there is always one person who is destined to rise above the madness and make it out. But when things go awry like the plans of mice and men, the hood suffers. When the community loses its glue, the citizens have no clue what to do!

Unfortunately, everyone relapsed when I passed away.

I was the hope and the fuel to their souls. My funeral is in a few days. This will be the toughest day in history to endure for the City of Bridgeton.

CHAPTER 16:
TWO PEAS

Who were we?
We were Two Peas

-Brother Brown

The day has come to bury me. Lost in his thoughts, and still swimming in his emotions, Pain is not holding up well. He is not ready to send me off, just yet. Pain's eyes are swollen from crying all week. Everyone is sort of upset with Pain because they think he is the reason for me dying. They feel as though if he would have never gone after the Mayor, then I would still be alive. When Pain goes through rough patches, I was always there for him to guide him through. With me out the way, he is just an emotional wreck. I tamed Pain, and now he is about to go off the deep end. He hasn't been eating lately either.

It's eight-thirty in the morning. Pain sits on his bed reminiscing on the good times we had when I was living.

Pain's mother knocks twice on his door. She instructs him to get ready for the funeral. Pain wipes his tears and glimpses up at his suit he is wearing today. An all-white suit hangs on the back of his door. Pain is sending me off in style! He really loved me. Pain is speaking at my funeral. I have no idea how that is going to go. I am sure he will say some kind words on my behalf.

Pain stands up and stretches. He opens the door to the sight of his mother. She leans in and attempts to embrace Pain. They embrace. She squeezes Pain tighter than he expected. He tightens his grip in return. Warm tears from his mother's face splash on his shoulders as she began to speak.

"I am so sorry for your loss, baby, stay strong and keep your head up. This day will be one of the hardest of your life. I know you are still in shock and everything seems unreal. Just pray and ask God for guidance. He will show you the way."

Pain nods but stays silent.

Pain heads to the bathroom. He washes his face and stares into the mirror. His eyes are bloodshot red. He takes a deep breath then reaches for his toothbrush.

The doorbell rings.

Pain still in his underwear and tank top hurries to finish brushing his teeth. He quickly runs back into his bedroom. He reaches behind his pillow and grabs his 9mm. He cocks it and proceeds to head to the door.

"Stay in your room!" he instructs his mother.

Pain isn't taking any chances. He won't let them take him that easy. He peeks through the peephole. He sees a silhouette but cannot recognize the face. He raises his weapon and simultaneously opens the door.

It's White Boy Al, dressed in an all-black suit. This is the cleanest he has ever looked. Pain exhales deeply.

"WOAH, WOAH, WOAH! It's me, bro! What the fuck?"

Pain quickly pulls Al inside the apartment. Then he pokes his head back out into the hallway. He looks left and then right, then quickly closes the door.

"My bad about that bro. Since they've killed Knowledge I have been paranoid out of my mind. I feel like I am next. I'm glad you are here. I need you to roll me a blunt.

Pain liked to smoke but never knew how to roll.

I need to calm my nerves before I head up in this church.

Honestly, I am not ready to see him go."

Al replied, "You good bro. I understand. I have been having a hard time dealing with this shit as well. We need to smoke a blunt ASAP, hence the reason I came here so early. It was hell getting up here though. You have all the cobras on guard inside and out of the building. This shit locked down like Fort Knox. They frisked me from head to toe. They eased up when one vouched and acknowledged me as the white boy who does your homework."

Pain looked outside his window. He sees his top enforcer pacing the entrance. He gets his attention with the cobra call.

"TSSSSSS"

The enforcer looks up.

"Aye, we are coming down soon. Stay alert and tell the cobras to tighten up!"

The enforcer nods and throws up the Cobra signal.

White Boy Al begins to break down the marijuana. Pain tells him to come into his room. He doesn't like to smoke in front of his mother. Once in Pain's room, Al heads for the desk to finish rolling the blunt. Pain puts on his all-white suit.

"Look at you, looking like a five dollar gallon of milk!"

Pain laughs. Once Pain is dressed he takes a seat on his bed.

Al sits in the rolling chair and lounges back. He pulls out a blue lighter and proceeds to light the blunt. He takes a long pull and exhales slowly.

The window in his room is still open.

Al hands Pain the blunt.

Pain inhales the blunt and exhales. He hits it again and begins to vent to Al.

"Bro I can't believe Knowledge is gone. I look at my phone and await his calls. My phone will never ring with his caller ID anymore! I want to knock on his door and invite him to go shoot around, but I know he isn't home. It is a weird feeling when you know you won't see someone again, and all you have is a plethora of memories playing in your mind like a movie."

"I feel the same way bro. Life will never be the same. I am not going to hold you, this some good ass weed."

Ten minutes go by and the blunt has evaporated. Pain closes the window and heads for the living room. Al follows. Pain's mother meets them in the living room and lets him know that she is ready.

"You two look nice", she says to us as she sprays perfume on herself.

Pain called his enforcer via FaceTime.

"Get the truck ready, we will be down in five minutes."

Pain grabs his 9mm and tucks it in his back. He grabs his house keys and motions, everyone, out the door. Before exiting, he picks up a picture of his father. He softly kisses the portrait. In a low tone he mumbles, "Watch over me pops, and show me the way."

Pain locks the door and they all make their way down the hallway towards the elevator. Halfway down the hallway, a door opens behind them. It's my parents. They step out and lock the door behind them. Pain, still paranoid, takes his hand off his weapon once he notices who he is looking at. They all embrace and head for the elevator as one.

They step out of the building. Two cars are parked in the front. One is a large escalade and the other is a black vehicle from the funeral home.

Pain tells his enforcer to fill the escalade with his wolves. When Pain speaks of his wolves, he is referring to a group of his most loyal and dangerous soldiers. In a span of seconds, six men appear and jump in the escalade. Pain instructs them to follow closely and not let any cars in between them en route to the funeral. Pain opens the door to the other vehicle. My parents jump in first. Then Al and Pain's mother enter. Pain is the last one to enter the car.

He gives the driver the "okay" to depart. The two-car convoy heads to the church, to attend my funeral.

Both cars arrive at the front of the church. Pain calls his enforcer and instructs him to have his wolves set up a perimeter around the car to ensure safe entry to pay their respects. The logistics were planned well. Pain didn't know if the mayor had anyone watching him, so he is playing offense in this situation. He can't afford to sit back and play defense at this point. The mayor already set the stage. The logic is 'kill or be killed' at this point. I understand it fully; I hope Pain gets that corrupt motherfucker.

An usher opens up the double doors to the church. The viewing of my body is still taking place. The line is long. The usher gestures to them to enter. Pain instructs two of his wolves to remain outside.

Pain points towards two of his wolves and says, "After you view the body come relieve these two so they can say their final goodbye. After that, I need all four all you to stand guard outside until the service is over. Call me if you need anything."

They nod, and then throw up the cobra sign.

They enter the church walking two by two. Pains enforcer and lieutenant lead the way. My parents are behind them; followed by Pain and his mother. Behind them are Al and his father. He was waiting outside the church when we arrived. The last two people in the line are the two wolves. Inside the church the atmosphere is sad. Sniffles and cries are heard from everywhere.

Pain and everyone waited in line to view me.

"He didn't deserve that. He died for nothing!" someone shouted out.

They arrive at my casket. The enforcer and the lieutenant both touch the four corners of their chess simultaneously. The pattern makes out a cross. They then split up to both sides of the casket as my parents approached. My mother is struggling to walk. She is not ready to see me like this, all pale and lifeless. My father helps escort her to see me. He has to stay strong for everyone even though he is suffering himself. My father has a stoic expression on his face. His face is full of tears as he observes me in silence. My mother has her head down. As she slowly lifts her head up, she sees me and loses it.

"NOOOOOOOOOOO! NOT MY BABY!'

" THEY KILLED MY ONLY BABY. HE WOULDN'T HURT ANYONE. HE WAS ONLY GOING TO THE STORE."

My father rubs her back as she continues to look on. Two minutes later he then escorts her to their seats on the front row. Pain steps up. His mother is rubbing his back gently.

"We love you, Knowledge!" someone yells out.

Pain takes a deep breath. His lips quiver as he struggles to get his thoughts together.

"Let it out baby.", Pain's mother says softly.

"AAAAAAAARGH! This shit hurts, man. I can't go on without you, bro. I love you, kid!"

Pain reaches inside his white suit jacket and pulls out a picture. It's the picture I took in the café that day we were rapping. He places it in my casket. He and his mother take their seats.

Al touches my hand and tells me he will see me later. He and his father sit next to Pain and his mother.

The viewing is over. Everyone takes their seats. The pastor walks to the podium and greets us with a quick prayer.

"Dear Lord. I come to you and ask you to pray over the Peters family in their time of need. Lord this family needs you more than anything. I trust that you will change the bulbs of the world and allow the people to see the light again. Let all the eyes be restored with vision and purpose. I pray that the violence will stop today. In Jesus' name amen."

The preacher takes a step back into the pulpit. An elderly lady walks to the microphone. A few seconds pass and a soft melody play in the background. She began to sing a beautiful song.

There is power in the name of Jesus To break every chain,
There's an army rising up to break every chain,
Break every chain,
Break every chain

The song brought the congregation to tears. She hit all the high notes and she received a standing ovation as she walked back to her seat.

The pastor gets back up and returns to the microphone at the pulpit.

"At this time we will have a poem read by Derrick Jackson. That's Pain's real name. Pain excuses himself as he scoots through the row he is sitting on. He adjusts his suit and heads for the microphone. He taps it to make sure it is properly working. It is.

Pain takes a deep breath and says, "This is extremely hard for me. Knowledge was my best friend. I am not good with speeches so I just decided to write a poem. I named it "Two Peas" because that's what we were."

He reaches in his suit jacket once again and pulls out a folded piece of paper. He cleared his throat and began to read off the wrinkled paper.

<u>TWO PEAS</u>

WE WERE RAISED TOGETHER
EVERY DAY WE PLAYED TOGETHER
ON THE WEEKENDS
WE STAYED TOGETHER
EVEN THOUGH LIFE WAS A STORM
WE ENJOYED THE WEATHER
WHO WERE WE?
WE WERE TWO PEAS

TWO PEAS IN A POD
WHO VOWED TO MAKE OUR LIVES EVEN
WE WERE DESTINED TO BEAT THE ODDS
NOTHING WAS GIVEN TO US
WE HAD TO EARN EVERYTHING
WE FEARED NOTHING

SEE, WE HAD A PLAN
A PLAN TO TAKE OVER
MY MARATHON MUST CONTINUE
EVEN THOUGH YOUR RACE IS OVER
I FEEL EMPTY WITHOUT YOUR PRESENCE
THINKING BACK
I AM THANKFUL FOR THE LESSONS
THROUGHOUT MY LIFE KNOWLEDGE
YOU HAVE TRULY BEEN A BLESSING

I DON'T KNOW HOW TO MOVE ON WITHOUT YOU
JUST KNOW I WON'T FORGET ABOUT YOU
KNOWLEDGE WAS MY BROTHER
FROM ANOTHER MOTHER
HE WAS THE ONLY ONE I TRUSTED

DON'T FEEL SORRY FOR ME
SAVE ME THE SORROW, PLEASE
I MISS YOU KNOWLEDGE

WHO WERE WE?
WE WERE
TWO PEAS

I'M SORRY FOR YOUR LOSS MR.T
YOU STILL HAVE A SON IN ME
I'M STILL NEXT DOOR IF YOU NEED ME
BELIEVE ME.
I'M HURTING

THIS PUNCH FROM LIFE JUST STUMBLED ME
MY LIFE WILL NEVER BE THE SAME
KNOWLEDGE REIGNED SUPREME

HE KNEW EXACTLY WHO HE WAS
HE KNEW EXACTLY WHERE HE WAS GOING
IN THE FIGHT OF LIFE
HE TOOK THE RIGHTEOUS STANCE

WHO WERE WE?
WE WERE TWO PEAS
WHO GREW FROM A SACRED POD
BUT
KNOWLEDGE WAS CUT FROM A DIFFERENT CLOTH
THAT FABRIC IS SOLD OUT ACROSS THE WORLD
HE WAS TRULY ONE OF A KIND

IN THIS POD WE CALL LIFE
WE LIVE AND WE LEARN
AFTER WE LEARN
IT'S TIME TO APPLY
THAT WAS KNOWLEDGE'S FAVORITE LINE
HE SAID IT ALL THE TIME
HIS MEMORIES WILL KEEP MY SPIRIT FULL
I WILL SMILE WHEN I THINK OF HIM

SO FOR THOSE WHO DON'T KNOW
WHO WE WERE

WE WERE TWO PEAS
TWO PEAS IN A POD
WHO TOOK AN OATH TO BEAT THE ODDS

REST IN PEACE KNOWLEDGE.

I LOVE YOU, BRO!

-PAIN

For fifteen seconds after the speech, the church was silent. Then one person clapped and broke the silence. Everyone stood to their feet and gave pain a standing ovation. That was a beautifully written poem. Pain should have that shit framed. As Pain exited the stage he hugged my parents and let them know everything was going to be okay.

My funeral ends and everyone is taking pictures and hugging. Pain's phone vibrates. He gets a text from one of his wolves that were outside on guard duty. The text reads "EMERGENCY." Pain rounds up everyone he came with and heads for the exit to see what the problem is.

Pain leads the group outside. Upon his arrival, he notices 5 black trucks parked back to back. His wolves brief him that the trucks just pulled up and have been sitting idle for about five minutes. The sound of a door unlocking is heard. Pain and all the cobras quickly place their hands on their weapons and watch the vehicles attentively.

All doors open. Fifteen men jump out and approach Pain, the cobras, and my parents.

"Who the fuck are you?" one cobra asks one of the suited men.

The men stood silent. The last truck door swings open and all eyes are glued on it. A black Stacy Adam is the first thing Pain sees get out the vehicle. Who could this be?

It's the motherfucking mayor.

He is dressed in all black. He ashes his cigar and makes his way to Pain. The pastor comes outside and tells my father to round up the pallbearers. It is almost time to carry me out. My father instructs the pastor that he will be there in a few minutes.

The mayor attempted to speak.

"Mr. and Mrs. Peters I am so-"

Pain cuts him off mid-sentence!

"You have some fucking nerve coming here. You must want to die. Save your condolences, we don't want to hear you're 'sorry.' You best get a vest and watch your back. This is war! I am coming for you with everything I have. I will not stop until I get you. And for them two bricks you are beat. Charge it to the game. Today I'm letting you slide Mr. Mayor. I just want to bury my best friend in peace. But rest assured, when the clock strikes midnight, war will be back in session. Now do us all a favor and get the fuck out of here!

The mayor smirks. His detail stands there sizing up the cobras, still silent.

"Like I tried to state earlier, I am sorry for your loss Mr. and Mrs. Peters. I send my condolences. This was all a misunderstanding, and I am sorry it went down like this."

The mayor tells his men to mount up, and as he walks off he tells Pain that he isn't ready to play with the big boys.
They pull off as quickly as they came.

They carry me out slowly and Pain talks to my casket.

"I will avenge this. You died for nothing, bro. I am about to bring the wrath like never before. Rest in peace, kid." says Pain as he pushes my casket in the back of the hearse.

Everyone arrives at my burial site. The preacher says a prayer and releases the doves into the air. Flowers are laid on my casket in the form of a cross. I'm lowered slowly into the ground to never be seen again. I guess this is the end.

Pain's enforcer pulls him to the side and lets him know that he is angry and ready to ride. He doesn't like how the situation played out. The arrogance of the mayor rubbed him wrong.

"So what's the plan boss?" he asks with emphasis

"I have it all figured out. I have a plan."

CHAPTER 17:
PEEWEE'S INTEL

Never underestimate the poor man's wisdom.

As soon as the clock struck midnight, Pain was back in war mode to avenge my death. Pain is the type of person who doesn't stop until he achieves his goal. Some say that is a weakness but not me. Consistency and perseverance breed resilience and that is a great trait to have in any situation. Pain receives a phone call from Peewee around 2 am.

"Peewee, I hear you're getting high again. Tell me that's not true."

"Yeah, I relapsed. It was tough to deal with the loss of Knowledge. That shit fucked me up. Don't let my actions make you think I forgot about the mission at hand."

There is an old saying that states, "never underestimate the poor man's wisdom. He is poor only by his decision-making but rich in life lessons. Failure has taught him more than success ever could."

"You must have some information for me, hence you calling me in the middle of the night."

"Yes, I have a way you can catch the mayor alone."

"I am listening. Give me the Intel you have gathered."

"I have been following him for the past few days. He runs a tight ship. He always has his detail with him. They roll five trucks deep no matter where they go. It's impossible to catch him during business hours. That's when I realized he must have a vice. To my surprise, he does no drugs, but he has a secret. He is into sadomasochism also known as BDSM. He likes to be tied up and have toys used on him. He is a real freak. I was at the hair salon the other day hustling and overheard some ladies gossiping about it. Basically, the Mayor is having an affair with this woman I used to date back in the day. I know where she lives and all that. She has a daughter your age and her name is Courtney, I believe. Anyway, they meet every Thursday at noon at her house. He comes alone because he doesn't want his wife to find out. Hotels are too risky because everyone knows his face. I guess that's why he goes to her house. I take nothing at face value. I sat out there and saw it for myself. He showed up at noon and left by 2 pm promptly."

"That's why I fuck with you, Peewee. I knew you were good for something," Pain says as he writes down the address.

"34 Hampton St Bridgeton, NJ 08302. Got it."

Most men have a vice that takes a toll on them. Some drink, smoke weed, and others trick off on pussy. Vices lead to most of our demise. We don't realize it until it's too late though. Now that Pain has the inside scoop, I wonder how he is going to go about avenging me. I bet you are too.

CHAPTER 18:
LAY LOW AND PLAY SLOW

The best place to hide is in plain sight.

Every other thought on Pain's mind is the Mayor. The marking period was almost over so he tried to attend school to get his mind clear. He couldn't use my death as an excuse for any more absences. His first day back, the history teacher was assigning partners for the final exam. Pain and Courtney were chosen to work together. The project they had to work on was a presentation about Malcolm X and his legacy via a PowerPoint presentation. White Boy Al already took this class and was willing to lend the presentation to Pain. Pain began to devise his plan. He studied the presentation and became familiar with the subject matter. Courtney allowed him over to work on the project on a Wednesday. The project was due Friday. Pain brought flowers as he approached the residence. Before he went and knocked on the door he made sure the address Peewee gave him was right and exact. It was.

Pain sent her a text to let her know he was outside. Courtney answered the door soon after. She was taken back by the flowers and started to blush.

"Oh my God, Pain, you shouldn't have.

Courtney motions him inside.

"It's only right that I partake in my role as the perfect gentleman," says Pain in a smooth voice.

Courtney begins to vent about her life and her problems. Pain had to play possum and entertain it.

"Pain I am so overwhelmed right now. SATs are coming up. All these projects are due soon. I also have to write a letter to the college I want to attend. Honestly, I am ready to graduate and be done with this shit. Cheerleading isn't the same without

Knowledge being on the court. How have you been holding up?"

Her eyes are watery. She couldn't hold it in any longer.

"I have been holding up to the best of my ability. It is hard to cope with. I miss him dearly. But I have good news for you. Christmas comes twice a year. I have our project already completed. I know it is hard to juggle many tasks at once. I hope my kind gesture relieves some of the pressure in your life. When we present on Friday all you have to do is read off the board when it's your turn."

Courtney is taken back once again. Pain is pulling out all his seductive courting tactics. He is going for the jugular. He states she has a nice home and she quickly gives him a tour of the residence. Pain is taking mental notes as to where everything is. Pain takes a special interest in the location of her mother's room. It was downstairs! After the tour, they returned to the kitchen table to practice the presentation. They get it down and Pain tells Courtney he likes her. She blushed. Pain then attempted to extract information from Courtney by picking her brain.

"So what college are you thinking about attending beautiful? Do you have any scholarships? College is expensive, don't go into debt if you don't have to." says Pain looking concerned.

"I am going to Spelman on a partial scholarship. My godfather is paying the rest of my tuition. I am blessed when it comes to having good people in my corner."

"Damn, your godfather must have that bag huh?"

"Duh, my godfather is the Mayor."

"The Mayor! Damn you are blessed. I wish you the best in all your endeavors."

Courtney nods. Pain lets her know he has to go and that he will see her in class on Friday.

"I have a doctor's appointment in the morning, so I won't be in school tomorrow."
Pain pulls out his phone and heads toward the door.

Pain calls his enforcer to pick him up. He instructs him to bring the wolves just in case someone followed him. Pain is playing offense. I told you he was smart.

"Courtney I really like you, we should stay in touch."

She blushes and states, "You have my number, use it more often!"

Pain is smooth as they come. Peewee was right. Everything checked out. Now all he has to do is devise a plan. Time is of the essence.

The Mayor's vice was his sexual desires. He was so much of an addict that he was cheating on his wife with a different woman. And to make things worse his dumb ass started claiming her kid as his own. To top it all off he was planning to spend a bag on her tuition all in the name of his vice. What part of the fucking game is that? Pussy is always more powerful than dick, in most cases.

Pain gets home and calls Courtney. He talks sweet nothings to her all night. She is under his spell now. When we were twelve years old we read "The Art of Seduction" and never forgot the lessons. So in the field of romance, Pain wears many hats. You never know what you are going to get with him.

"I have enjoyed our conversation tonight. I am glad I finally shot my shot. I have to get some rest now. The sun shall rise again my queen. I will see you soon. Stay black and stay beautiful. One love, Pain."

I told you he was smooth as glass. Honestly, he is the smoothest person I have seen since I looked in the mirror! Let me stop.

CHAPTER 19:
COBRA STRIKE

Like the cobra, you remain coiled in a loose but compact position and your strike should be felt before it is seen.

-Bruce Lee

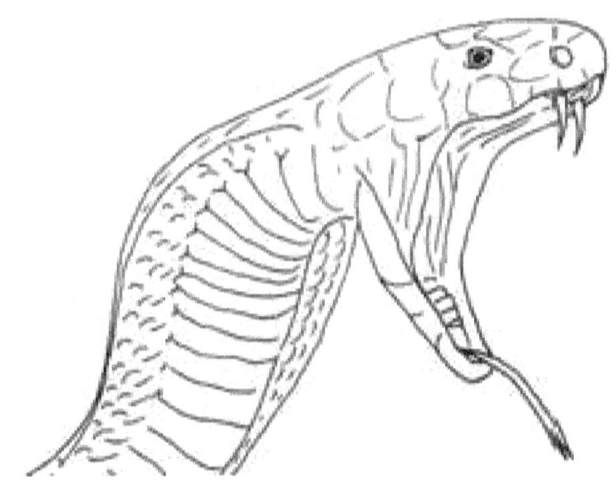

Thursday came quick. Pain wakes up and goes through his morning routine as he prepares for school. He wakes up to a good morning text from Courtney. She is deep into his Venus flytrap. She is not aware of the spell that has been cast. He replied he will call her after he leaves the doctor around two o'clock. He told her the doctor's office was far away. That was the reason he would be missing the whole day of school. The perfect alibi seed has been planted. Pain tells his mother that she is loved as he heads out the door. As soon as he exits the building, he jumps into the truck with his enforcer. It is 8 am at this point.

"So what's the plan boss?" the enforcer asks Pain while rubbing his hands together.

"I recently got the scoop on the Mayor. I have found a weak link in his operation chain. I have the address and a solid alibi. I can handle him myself. I just need you to keep the car running while I handle my handle. We have a few hours to kill, so let's go get some breakfast. Take me to Denny's."

"Coming right up."

As they arrive, they check the perimeter to ensure safety. The coast was clear. As they sat down to eat, Pain lays down the game plan to execute the mission. He goes over the plan many times to ensure everything goes right. Once he feels like all doubt is ceased, Pain pays the bill and they all head back to the vehicle. The time is now 10:30 am.

"Take me to this address. I need you to park in the alley a few streets back. You can see the house from there. Let me know when they pull up," instructs Pain.

The enforcer nods.

They arrive at exactly 11 am. Pain goes to the side of the house and breaks in the bedroom window. They must've forgotten to turn the alarms on this morning. Pain looks around for the closet in Courtney's mother's room. To his surprise, it was a huge walk-in closet with plenty of room to hide. The closet door had cuts on it to allow him to see clearly into the bedroom. The bed lay in front of him. He checks his watch and realizes he has thirty minutes until they arrive. He put on white latex gloves and screwed a black silencer on his 9mm. He pulls out a piece of paper from his pocket. It's the quote that Peewee gave him. He says to himself:

I am a King
I will reign forever on The Hill.
Pain is my name
That is all I bring
My trauma fuels my spirit tank.
May I never run out of gas!

Moments later Pain hears the front door open. The sounds of kissing and fondling are heard from the closet where he is hiding. The sound of wine entering wine glasses is heard as well. Pain receives a text from his enforcer.

"The mayor is in the house. He has a black suit on with a blue tie. He is alone. He is with the woman whom you described at breakfast. I guess she picked him up from a prior location. I can see their bedroom from where I am parked. See you soon. *TSSS*"

Pain doesn't reply. They burst into the bedroom. They can't keep their hands off each other. The Mayor quickly undressed Courtney's mother. She was thick as fuck. Her breasts were perked up and her nipples were hard. I see why he stepped out on his wife. Pain is watching attentively from the closet. His nine is already out and cocked.

She began to speak, "Did you file for divorce yet? You've been saying you were going to do it for the past month. Why are you dragging your feet? You said you want to be with me, don't you?"

"I am working on it. I am here for a limited time. Let us not waste countless minutes conversing about a divorce. You know what I came to do. Go get the bag, my love!

He takes off his suit and gets ass naked. Then gently lays the suit on the floor. I guess he didn't want to wrinkle it. Pain was relieved he didn't come in the closet for a hanger. It's 12:30 now. Pam, which is the name of Courtney's mother, according to the mayor quickly returned to the room with a black gym bag. Music plays from a speaker in the room. Smooth R&B Jazz instrumentals fill the atmosphere. I guess this is how the old folks get down.

First, she pulled out handcuffs and handcuffed the mayor's hands to both sides of the headboard posts, then proceeded to blindfold him with a scarf. She pulled out a feather and began to play with his nipples. Pam returned to the bag of toys and pulled out a gag ball and tied it around his head. The mayor tried to speak but she smacked him and told him to shut up.

"I am in charge here, I don't want to hear another peep out of you bitch!"

"This nigga supposed to be the plug and the most feared man in town. He in here getting his nipples ticked with a fucking ball in his mouth. He is a whole nut out here! The cobras aren't going to believe this shit," says Pain to himself still distraught at what he is looking at.

Pain's heart is beating fast. He isn't accustomed to breaking in houses.

A knock comes from the front door. She looks outside and doesn't recognize the face. Surprised by the random visit, Pam quickly throws on a robe to answer the door. She leaves the mayor tied to the bed still gagged and blindfolded.

"Baby, I will be right back. Let me see who the hell this is."

The mayor nods.

She answers the door. It's Peewee disguised as a delivery guy! He has a pizza in his hand. Pam is confused because she didn't order the pizza.

"Hello, here is your cheese pizza, Mrs. Watkins. Thank you for shopping with us."

"This is the Kings' residence, sir. The Watkins live next door."

"Oh, please forgive me, I am so sorry. Enjoy the rest of your day."

While all that was taking place at the front door, Pain sprung into action. He opened the closet door slowly. He then proceeded to lock the door of the bedroom. The mayor senses the presence of a human in the room and becomes quickly aroused. He thinks it is Pam returning. Pain grabs the feather off the ground and aims for the nipples of the mayor. He jumps up and wiggles his toes. He likes that shit for real I see. Pam makes her way back to the room. She reaches for the doorknob and attempts to turn it. Pain can hear her talking to herself.

"Damn baby, I locked myself out. I have an extra key in the garage. I will be right back."

The mayor mumbles some jargon. It's 1:15 pm now. The sound of

Pam's footsteps soon fades away. Pain punches the mayor in the face then smacks him with his gun. He begins to scream but the music wipes out the sound. Pain untied the blindfold slowly and stepped back. Pain then aimed at the mayor's head. Once the mayor's eyes adjusted to the light, he was surprised to see Pain! His eyes grew wide as he realized he was at the mercy of his once business partner, turned enemy.

"Yeah, surprise motherfucker! I caught you with your draws down. Look at you now, Old freak nasty ass motherfucker! I have to give it to you though. You had a good run, but that all ends now. You killed my father, you killed my best friend, and you tried to kill me! I would take the ball out of your mouth and hear your final words but I could care less what you have to say at this point. Nobody can save you now. Vices killed you; See if you had been faithful I wouldn't have had this opportunity to catch you slipping. You have to know how to control that thing down their sir. Sex is powerful and sacred, and you are out here tricking like it's no tomorrow! YOU SHOULD BE ASHAMED OF YOURSELF."

The mayor squirms as he attempts to free himself from the cuffs. He is helpless. Pain aims at the mayor's head. He tightens the silencer until it doesn't turn to the right anymore. He took a deep breath and then pulled the trigger.

Tss. Tss. Tss.

Three rounds exited the chamber and entered the flesh of the mayor; two shots to the chest and one in the head.

Execution-style. I didn't think Pain had it in him. I mean he has shot many people, but he never killed anyone.

Pain picked up the shell casings then opened the window.

Through the music, he could hear footsteps coming up the steps. Pam must've found her spare key. Pain picked up the quote from the floor and jumped out the window. He closes the window and bolts towards the truck with his enforcer waiting. Once at the car, Peewee is in the backseat eating pizza. The same pizza he was supposed to be delivering! He has to be the illest cobra ever. The sound of a woman screaming is heard in the near distance. Pam has just discovered the corpse of the mayor.

The enforcer pulls out slowly and drives off. He doesn't want the tires to screech. That's how you get caught. Peewee gets out in the alley so he can hide in plain sight. He wants to obtain all information from the investigation just in case Pain made a mistake.

Pain received a text from Sweets, which read that he has a signed doctor's note for him. Sweets had a doctor on his team that would do anything for him. Pain's alibi is solidified!

"How you feeling man, I know this was a huge task. You handled it like a gangster. I am proud of you."

"I got him. I shot that motherfucker in his head. He is gone. I still feel empty though. I am still lonely in a sense. I thought avenging my father and Knowledge would bring peace to me. I still feel the same. Do you have any advice?"

"I have killed many people. It never gets easy. You just have to keep pushing on. Live your life is all I can say. What is done is done though. You can't go back and change things."

Kenneth Whalum said it best in this one song I like. He states,

I won't tell you that it's going to be ok

Those were powerful words the enforcer quotes. Pain texts Courtney and lets her know that he is on his way back in town and wants to see her. Pain is dropped off at his building and he heads upstairs. He sees my father in the hallway. My father has lost a lot of weight after losing me. Pain nods at him and says, "It's finished Mr. T" and my father nods back and heads towards the elevator. Pain's phone rings. It's Courtney. She is hysterical!

"Pain someone killed my godfather. I don't think I can see you today. I have to go. I don't want you to think I was dodging you. Talk to you later, baby."

Courtney hangs up.

Pain took a shower and then changed his clothes. He bags up the outfit from the crime into a gym bag. He carries it outside and hands it off to one of the cobras. The weapon was in the bag as well. He then gets a ride to my gravesite and rests his hand on my tombstone, then begins to speak. Tears fell from his eyes. Pain is as tough as they come, but this time in his life is a true test of adversity.

Knowledge. I miss you kid. I miss the tough love you gave. I miss the random history facts you used to drop on me. I miss your positive energy. I am sorry you died. Sometimes I feel like I should have died that day. I still get nightmares. I wake up in cold sweats sometimes. I lost all motivation to go on in life. When you were here we had a plan, now that you are gone I am just lost out here. You can finally rest in peace; I killed the mayor for you. He is gone, and will never return. You know I am not big on religion, but please watch over me as I continue on. Send me a sign from time to time. Show me you are watching over me. I know you are in heaven dunking on everyone on those heavenly courts. I know you don't drink alcohol so I brought you a Gatorade. Here's some for you. I know you need it up there. I love you Knowledge, I will see you when they get me.

One Love from your other half,

With Love,

-Pain

CHAPTER 20: GRADUATION (THE SURPRISE)

Life and time are forever running. They stop for no man. Make your mark while you are here.

-Brother Brown

Two years later the big day has come, high school graduation! White Boy Al and Pain are sitting in the auditorium taking pictures in their caps and gowns. I'm proud of Pain. He stuck it out and finished strong. He could have easily slipped deeper into the dark side but he fought hard and won. He has been going to counseling to help cope with my absence. Two years later he still feels empty with me not around.

"Pain on some real shit, I'm very proud of you. You have come a long way and I just want to commend you. Keep it up," says White Boy Al.

"I couldn't have done it without you bro. I have to tell you something. I have a surprise for you." Says Pain reaching in his pocket.

White Boy Al sat there waiting eagerly to see what the news was.

"Good Luck at Harvard, Al," says one of the graduates as she walks past.

It was a given that White Boy Al was going to make it out the hood. His foundation was solid. I wish him the best in all his endeavors.

"Read this bro! I wanted you to be the first to know!" says Pain smiling.

White Boy Al takes the folded sheet of paper and begins to read it.

Clark Atlanta University
Office of Admissions

Dear Derrick Jackson,

I am delighted to inform you that you have been offered an opportunity to attend Clark Atlanta University on a full scholarship. We are lucky to have a student of your caliber on our campus. We look forward to seeing you in the fall. We are sure our business program will prepare you for success in all your endeavors.

Congrats Again,

Dr. Dave Barter

404-880-8000

Clark Atlanta University

"Find a way or make one"

White Boy Al is taken back by what he just read. A single tear races to his chin as he embraces Pain. No one had seen this coming, not even me.

"Man, that's what's up bro. I am elated to hear that you are taking life by the horns. Knowledge would be proud of you. I know he is up there smiling," says White Boy Al as he wipes his tears of happiness away.

"Yeah, he would. He would be proud of you too. We will keep his name alive. Come on; let's go line up. It's time to walk the stage and make our families proud."

The bleachers were packed as the graduates came out towards the stadium. They cheered loudly and clapped as the graduates walked by waving and smiling. The principal gave a nice speech and then started to call the names of the graduates.

Pain and Al were right behind each other in line waiting to be called. Pain was nervous.

"My feet hurt in these damn Stacy Adams. I am used to wearing my Jordan's," says Pain.

White Boy Al chuckled as Pain stepped up to be awarded his diploma.

"Derrick Lamar Jackson," says the announcer.

The stadium erupted in cheers as Pain waved on. Lost in the moment Pain takes off his gown. Under his gown, he had on a shirt with my face on it. Under the picture, it said congratulations grad. Still lost in the moment, he headed to the announcer and grabbed the microphone, and looked into the sky.

"We did it, kid! We fucking graduated. Excuse my French y'all, but this here is for Knowledge. I need you all to stand on your feet and give my brother the love he deserves. He was supposed to be here with me today graduating. On the count of three, I need everyone to say 'Long Live Knowledge!'"

"One, two, three," counts Pain.

"LONG LIVE KNOWLEDGE!" yells the crowd.

"Again," yells Pain

"LONG LIVE KNOWLEDGE!" repeats the crowd.

"One more time for the road!" instructs Pain.

"LONG LIVE KNOWLEDGE!" yells the crowd one last time.

"I LOVE YOU, KNOWLEDGE!" screams Pain as he returns the microphone to the announcer. On his way back to his seat he spots my father in the crowd and points to him. The cobras have a small portion of the stadium full. Pain throws up the cobra signal and all the cobras let out a "TSSSSSSSSSS" that could be heard around the world. They were honored to see their general accomplish goals and set the standard of the organization.

As Pain sat down he heard his mother screaming, "I love you Pain, that's my son y'all."

Sitting back down, Pain is in good spirits. He will always keep my name alive any chance he gets. Loyal to the soil he is. Everyone is telling Pain how dope his speech was.

"Bro that shit was epic! Man, I am speechless. You are going to' change the world. You are like a reincarnated Knowledge," says White Boy Al sarcastically.

"Thanks, bro, but those are some big shoes to fill. I'll just focus on being a better me. I'll leave the rest up to God," says Pain.

Who were we?
We were Two Peas!

PASS OR FAIL?

All or nothing....

The due date soon arrives. I hand over my paper and I sit there and wait quietly as Dr. Banks begins to read. I hope he doesn't flunk me. I can't afford to take this class over. I would literally die.

Thirty minutes pass.

Dr. Banks finishes my assignment and is astonished. He is speechless as he glances up at me.

"What do you think, sir?" I ask nervously

"This paper is the perfect representation of the task that you were assigned. I have to know who you were in the story. If I had to take a guess, I would say you were Knowledge, which was the main character. You will receive an A for this masterpiece by the way."

"I was every character in the story, sir. Let me explain. Some days I am Knowledge, and some days I am Pain. These two personalities reside within my subconscious mind. They clash every second of my existence. It has been a tough battle deciding who rules my perception. Knowledge passed away early. The pressures and stereotypes of the world killed him along with his dreams. Now I am Pain, a rebel who opposes everything. The persona of Pain is the only one that remains. Who else can I be?

"Besides them, there are other personas that fight to control me as well.

"Some days I feel like Sweets, smooth and witty. Pimps are very charismatic, and I have a way with words.

"Some days I am Peewee, a wise man that is knowledgeable about how the world works with no resources to better my situation. Drugs got the best of me for a short period in my life. I won the war though.

"Some days I am Poppy, I don't want to deal with people whom I don't know personally. New friends are always the reason an empire goes down.

"Some days I am Reggie. I want to smoke and escape the physical realm momentarily. Marijuana is illegal, and the citizens of the working world deem the people who use it heathens.

"Some days I am Jersey. I go into 'hustle' mode and sell anything I can get my hands on.

Some days I am White Boy Al. I can complete tasks effortlessly when I put my mind to them, but sometimes I hang with the wrong crowd.

Some days I am Detective Clark. I will walk off the job in a heartbeat if I sense shit getting fishy, or if I don't like how I am being used.

Some days I am the Mayor. I have days where I think about all the things I've been through and say fuck the world. My way or the high way is the motto. Everyone suffers these particular days. He had to die!

"I was present during many barbershop debates growing up. That is the only place us men can go to seek counsel. That is our place of refuge.

"I was the speaker at most of my childhood friend's funerals. I was the one who stopped crimes from happening. I could not save everyone though. I realized that death was pointless in project politics. There had to be a better way to communicate without violence.

"So, in conclusion, the human experience is one like no other. You have to walk in one's shoes to get a full understanding of their reality. This story couldn't portray half of what I really experienced. I have seen life and lived life from many angles. I hope now you understand that life hits us all on many levels outside these school halls. Next time you see a student struggling with attendance and homework, I hope you don't result in automatically flunking them. For example, when you ask me to chime in on how I feel about Trump and his charges about treason, I can't focus on the lecture because I am too busy thinking about my friends and family who died for no reason! I know nobody cares, but this life is just not fair. They say we have to play the cards we were dealt, but they never question the shady dealers who keep giving us bad hands. The game is rigged. When gambling at the table of life, it is impossible to walk away unscathed."

I clear my throat and continue to defend my thesis.

"The world turns fast, and us black men barely get water breaks as we run our marathons. We only can rest when we die. It is true when they say us men were cursed to work by the sweat of our brows. It's a shame. In the world of philosophy, there are no wrong answers! So that means I am right in this case. Lastly, when I pass on my legacy will be that I fought life with everything I had, and I went down with my fist up. Let everyone know I fought until the end. I will be remembered as a righteous warrior who rebelled for the people. In layman's terms, I died trying to figure this shit out! I see no other way to live, sir.

"Thank you for the A. I am glad you liked the story! The cat is out of the bag with me. You already know who I am. So, who battles within you?"

Dr. Banks stood speechless.

I just messed up his psyche. He will never forget my story! Neither will you! Thanks for reading my book!

One Love,

Brother Brown

GUESS WHAT?

I know you didn't want the story to end. Neither did I. Here is an introduction to *Two Peas Part 2: The Story of Pain.* You are welcome.

TWO PEAS PART II:
The Story of Pain

Written By:
Jamal Brown

SYNOPSIS

Pain is heading off to attend Clark Atlanta University and leaving the hill to better his life. He is determined to make something of himself to honor his best friend Knowledge who was slain a few years ago. With new levels come new devils. Will Pain stay the course or will he revert back to his old ways as a ruthless rebel?

If a man tells you he is second-guessing himself and pondering giving up on his dreams, you now have to now think three times as hard when considering employing him to support yours. Never take anyone seriously who doesn't take themselves seriously.

-Basil Hibbert

INTRODUCTION

Peace. Welcome to my world. My name is Pain. I'm sure Knowledge told you all about me. It's been two years since he has passed away. I miss him dearly, but life goes on you know. I graduated high school last week. Shit was bittersweet. I had the entire crowd screaming his name. At this point, I bet you are wondering what is my next move huh? I am wondering that same question. I leave for college in a few days. I have to walk away from running the Cobras. I have to give the throne to my enforcer to run the hill while I am gone. He has been by my side through the roughest times. I'm sure he will lead my organization in the right direction. I'm having a going away party tonight. The entire neighborhood will be in attendance to send me off.

The night falls. The Hill is packed out with all the major players. I'm fresh to death; you know how I get down. I'm wearing a custom *Better Days* sweater, with the Jordan's to match. Earlier I received a fresh haircut, compliments of Nate. Oh yeah, I forgot to mention the custom cobra logo on the front of my sweater to represent the crew.

Nigga We Made It by Drake plays through the speakers. Cars honk as they battle for parking spots. Ladies are out in abundance and love is in the air. Ribs, chicken, and burgers are being barbecued, dice are being thrown, and blunts are being passed around. This is one of those golden moments I will never forget. White Boy Al just walked up. I guess we are celebrating together. He leaves the same day I do. We dap up each other and we post up on Sweets Cadillac.

"Go conquer the world young king, we are going to hold this down for you," says Peewee as he walks up to me.

Peewee has been doing well since the death of Knowledge. He is still off of drugs and now works for the City of Bridgeton. He and Roxanne are still together as well.

Sweets strolled up fresh to death as usual.

"Pain, I got people in Atlanta. Let me know if you get led astray. I'm here to guide you. Here is $200 to get some groceries in that dorm room when you land. Oh yeah Det. Clark is looking for you. Speaking of the devil. There he goes right there," says Sweets pointing with his eyes.

Detective Clark walks up. He is wearing a Nike sweatsuit and carrying a gift bag.

"Pain, congrats on finishing high school. I just wanted to send you off with my best wishes. I believe in you kid. You are smart. You can do anything you put your mind towards."

"Thanks, Detective. I won't let the city down. I will set the example. I haven't seen you patrolling lately. You still work for the police department?" asks Pain.

"No. I quit a few months ago. I work construction with my cousin. My offer still stands though. If the cobras need employment, let me know," says Detective Clark.

"I got you. Thanks again Detective Clark," says Pain

"It's Mr. Clark now. Miss me with the police talk."

I didn't see that coming at all from him. I'm glad he wised up.

Anyways, I jumped up on top of Sweets Cadillac. I tell everyone to listen up. I prepared a speech to enlighten everyone while I am gone.

I received an incoming call from Curtis. He was calling to let me know he was close to arriving at my party.

"I'll see you when you get here. Let me call you back though, Courtney is calling me," I say before I click over.

"What's the deal, beautiful, where are you? I can't celebrate without my Queen. I need you here before I give my speech," I say as I continue to stand on Sweet's car.

"Hush, I just got here. I see your picklehead ass. I'm walking to you now baby," says Courtney before she hangs up.

If you haven't put two and two together, Courtney and I are now dating. I made her my girlfriend shortly after I killed the mayor. I decided to fund her college education myself. She was destined for greatness and I want my investment to pay off. She is in her junior year over at Spelman. She flew up to fly back down with me to Atlanta. Her mother wasn't charged with the murder due to the fact that the detectives found no weapon and there wasn't any blood splatter on her. They did find the window open, but no fingerprints were found. The investigation is still open.

"How's my King Cobra doing? Is he ready to walk away from his kingdom?" asks Courtney as she and I embrace to kiss.

"It's my first time leaving the hood. I spent my entire life running the cobras and protecting Knowledge. I think it is time for me to reinvent myself," I say as I make my way back on top of Sweets car.

"Listen up. Let me give you all a history lesson on the Cobras. The Egyptians, kings, and pharaohs wore the cobra in the middle of their foreheads. A cobra has no eyelids; therefore it doesn't blink, meaning it never sleeps. A cobra is very alert and knows who its natural enemies are. With that being said, in my absence please don't lose the cobra way. Stay safe and vigilant. I am a phone call or flight away. Big Nuke will be in charge of running things while I am gone. If anyone gives him any problems, you will have to answer to me. I shouldn't have to remind you that Pain is my name and that's all I bring. You all should know that already. In conclusion, I want to thank everyone for coming. Food and drinks are free, complimentary of the cobras. Be safe and thanks again. COBRA FOR LIFE! *TSSSSSS!*"

The entire crowd replied with the Cobra call. I take care of my team. They love me and I love them. We are really all we got.

The party ended in peace as everyone said their final goodbyes. Peewee helped me clean up after everyone left. He is vital to the community like Knowledge once said.

"Thank you Peewee. Here goes a few dollars to show my gratitude," I say as I hand over two twenty-dollar bills.

"I did that out of my loyalty and love to the cobras. But hey, who am I to turn down free money? I'll use that to get some groceries for the house. Good Luck young man. I am proud of the man that you have become and I am anxious to see what you will become, in the long run," says Peewee as he pulls me in for a hug. Courtney and I make our way to the truck that Big Nuke my enforcer is waiting in. I open the door for her then I enter. Big Nuke drops us off at my spot. Before I get out of the vehicle, I tell him that I am going rogue. I am not coming out of the house until it is time to head to the airport. Only call me if there is an emergency.

The day of the flight comes. All our bags are packed as we wait for our ride to the airport. My mother made a huge breakfast. Eggs, biscuits, sausages, potatoes, and orange juice were the items on the menu. After I ate, I received a text from Big Nuke saying that he was outside. I hug my mother and tell her that I will call when I land.

"Mom, you hold it down while I am gone. You are the best mother a son could ask for. I'm going to conquer the world. One Love," I say I hug and kiss her on the cheek.

I open the trunk and toss all our bags inside. We sped off en route to the Philadelphia Airport. Our flight was scheduled for 1 pm. We arrived around 11 am. They recommend that we arrive two hours early. We arrive at our terminal and guess who is sitting down with three suitcases?

 It's Curtis!

"What's up bro, what are you doing up here?" I ask as I shake his hand.

"What's up, G? I'm going to college. I was accepted into Clark Atlanta University as well. I am going to major in Psychology. I was going to tell you at the party but I got too drunk and shit. But yeah, that's why I am here," he says as he makes his way back to his seat.

"Damn, that's dope kid," I say as I sit next to him.

Curtis and I chopped it up for about an hour and a half. We talked about what to expect and a little about our individual goals.

"Flight 102 to Atlanta is now boarding for zone three, Flight 102 to Atlanta is now boarding for zone three," says the lady at the desk scanning tickets.

We scan our tickets and make our way to our seats. We all sat together. I pulled out my phone and instructed everyone to smile for a picture.

Atlanta here we come.

To be continued...

My Ghetto Gospel

Even now,
I get discouraged
I wonder if they take it all back
would I still keep the courage?

I refuse to be a role model
I set goals,
Take control,
And drink out of my own bottles

I make mistakes
But learn from everyone
and when it's all said and done
I bet this brown brother will be a better one

If I upset you,
Don't stress,
Never forget,
That God isn't finished with me yet

I feel his hand on my brain
when I write books,
I go blind,
And let the Lord do his thing.

- Brother Brown (Inspired by Tupac Shakur)

STAY IN TOUCH

If you would like to get in touch with me, you can contact me on the following platforms.

Instagram: Brotherbrown856
Facebook: Brother Brown The Author
Snapchat: Spcbrown
Twitter: @mali_gee23
EMAIL: BROTHERBOWNTHEAUTHOR@GMAIL.COM
Website: www.brotherbrowntheauthor.com

If you enjoyed reading this book, drop a review on Amazon, Goodreads, and all other reading platforms to share your opinion with the world. Thanks in advance.

Here is your flower while you can smell it!

One Love,

Brother Brown

2 6 MILES

MY MARATHON
BY JAMAL BROWN

This book contains poems, notes, and short stories that describe my thought processes at various points in my life which pertain to a host of different situations. Through the good times and the bad times, I survived to tell the tale. FROM MY MARATHON TO YOURS, PACE YOURSELF!

AVAILABLE NOW FROM BROTHERBROWN PUBLISHING

26 MILES ________________________________ $20.00
TWO PEAS (PB) ___________________________ $20.00
TWO PEAS (HC) ___________________________ $35.00

EMAIL YOUR ORDER TO BROTHERBOWNTHEAUTHOR@GMAIL.COM

OR MAIL IN A MONEY ORDER WITH THE ORDER FORM BELOW TO JAMAL BROWN PO BOX 682861, MARIETTA, GA 30067

QTY	BOOK TITLE	COSTS	SUBTOTAL (QTY x COSTS)
	SHIPPING (FLAT RATE)	$7	$7.00
	TOTAL		$

MALX PRESENTS: STAY SOLID The Mixtape and STAY SOLID 2
MALX
STAY SOLID
The Mixtape
STAY 2 SOLID
GO DOWNLOAD!
IG: @Malxbtw_x2   Email: Sbmalx@icloud.com

10% OFF 1ST TIME CLIENTS!!
A Hicks
IN-HOME & MOBILE SPA
April Hicks
(Licensed Esthetician)
FACIALS
Mini Facial (30 min) $40
Relaxation Facial (45 min) $50
Acne Treatment Facial (1hr) $65
Anti-Aging Facial (1hr) $75
Microdermabrasion (45 min) $50
ULTRASONIC CAVITATION (PER SESSION)
(30 min) $40
4 Session Package $120
ADDITIONAL
Hand Treatment (15 min) $10
Foot Treatment (20 min) $15
Back Treatment (1hr) $50
SPECIALS!!!
Facial/Hand & Foot Treatment (1 hr 20 min) $75
Facial/Back Treatment (1 hr 30 min) $95
Facial/Back/Hand & Foot Treatment (1 hr 45 min) $120
Facial/Body Polish (2 hrs) $150
*Add Body Butter Rub $165
For Appointments, please call
(678) 507 - 8056 or Email: amerin0407@gmail.com

EXCLUSIVE
PROPERTY SOLUTIONS
KADEEM WILLIAMS
Owner
Anderson Sc
8645205518-(office)
8646238134-(cell)
exclusivepropertysolution.com
kwilliams@exclusivepropertysolution.com
FOR ALL YOUR REAL ESTATE NEEDS, TELL HIM BROTHERBROWN SENT YOU.

**SHOP "BETTER DAYS" CLOTHING
TELL THEM BROTHER BROWN THE AUTHOR
SENT YOU FOR A DISCOUNT!**